MARS

THE GOLDEN AGE

ISBN-13: 978-1-943466-05-4
ISBN-10: 1-943466-05-X

For those who dream of other worlds,
and for those who will one day visit them.

FEATURED WRITERS

Stephen Bartholomew
Frederic Brown
Frank W. Coggins
Dean Evans
Charles E. Fritch
Randall Garrett
Arthur G. Hill
Bascom Jones, Jr.
Tom Leahy
Vernon L. McCain
Kris Neville
Rog Phillips
Jack Sharkey
Robert J. Shea
Mari Wolf

Table of Contents

FIRST CONTACT

The Hitch Hikers

by Vernon L. McCain

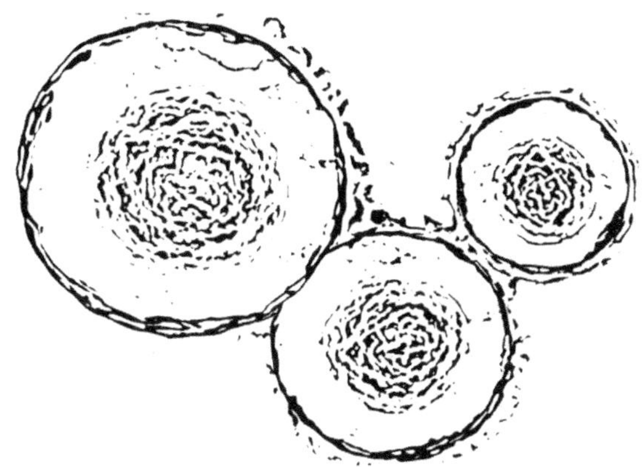

The dehydration of the planet had taken centuries in all. The Rell had still been a great race when the process started. Construction of the canals was a prodigious feat but not a truly remarkable one. But what use are canals when there is nothing left to fill them?

What cosmic influences might have caused the disaster baffled even the group-mind of the Rell. Through the eons the atmosphere had drifted into space; and with it went the life-giving moisture. Originally a liquid paradise, the planet was now a dry, hostile husk.

The large groups of Rell had been the first to suffer. But in time even the tiny villages containing mere quadrillions of the submicroscopic entities had found too little moisture left to satisfy their thirst and the journey ever southward toward the pole had commenced.

The new life was bitter and difficult and as their resources were depleted so also did their numbers diminish.

Huddled at their last retreat the Rell watched the ever smaller ice cap annually diminish and lived with the knowledge they faced extinction. A mere thousand years more would see even this trifling remainder gone.

Oh, you might say there was hope—of a sort. There might be Rell in the northern hemisphere. The canals girdled the globe and a similar ice cap could well exist at the opposite pole. Rell perhaps survived there also.

But this was scant comfort. The fate of the Rell in the south was sealed. What hope of any brighter future for those in the north? And if they survived a few hundred thousand years longer—or if they had perished a similar period earlier—what actual difference did it make?

There was no one more aware of this gloomy future than Raeillo/ee13.

In the old days a single unit of the group-mind of the Rell would have possessed but a single function and exercised this function perhaps a dozen times during his life. But due to the inexorable shrinkage only the most important problems now could command mind-action and each unit had been forced to forsake specialization for multi-purpose endeavors.

Thus Raeillo/ee13 and his mate Raellu//2 were two of the five thousand units whose task was to multiply in any group-mind action involving mathematical prediction. Naturally Raeillo/ee13 and Raellu//2 did not waste their abilities in mundane problems not involving prediction. Nor did they divide, add, or subtract. That was assigned to other units just as several million of the upper groups had the task of sorting and interpreting their results. Raeillo/ee13 and Raellu//2 multiplied only. And it must be admitted they did it very well. It is a pity the Rell could not have multiplied physically as easily as Raeillo/ee13 and Raellu//2 multiplied mentally.

With the exception of an occasional comet or meteor the Rell were seldom diverted by anything of a physical nature. The ice cap was their sole concern.

But one afternoon a rare physical phenomenon was reported by a bank of observer Rell.

"In the sky's northwest portion," an excited injunction came through. "Observe that patch of flaming red!"

More observer Rell were quickly focused on the novel sight and further data was rapidly fed into the interpretive bank.

The Rell were justifiably proud of their interpreters. With the race shrinkage it had proved impossible to properly train new interpreters. So, not without a great deal of sacrifice, the old interpreters, dating back to when the canals still flowed with water, had been kept alive.

They were incredibly ancient but there was no doubt as to their ability. It was a truism among the Rell that the interpretive banks arrived at their conclusions faster than any other group and that these conclusions could be checked to hundreds of decimal places without finding inaccuracy.

So it was no surprise to have the interpretive bank respond almost instantly, "It is quite odd but the flame appears to be of artificial origin."

"Artificial!" came the rough and questing probe of the speculative bank. "But how could Rell possibly be out there?"

"Who mentioned Rell?" was the interpretive bank's smug answer. They were not utterly averse to demonstrating their superior mental abilities on occasion.

The speculative bank replied, "Artificial implies intelligence, and intelligence means Rell."

"Does it?" the interpretive bank interrupted. The speculative bank waited but the interpretive bank failed to enlarge on the provocative query.

The Rell had found certain disadvantages accrued to abnormal prolongation of life and thus were not unused to the interpretive bank's occasional tendency to talk in riddles.

"Perhaps not," the speculative bank replied after a quick check with the logical formulae held in reserve by the historical bank. "It is theoretically possible that Rell-like individuals might have developed elsewhere, and perhaps even have developed intelligence, although, according to the historical bank, such an idea has never before been subjected to consideration. But what is the flame doing?" they continued, a trifle resentful at having been left to do work properly in the interpretive bank's province.

The observation and interpretive banks once more came into play, studying the situation for several minutes. "The flame appears to be the exhaust of a fairly crude vessel," the interpretive bank finally reported, "propelled by ignition of some gaseous mixture."

"Is it moving?"

"Quite rapidly."

"Where is it going?"

This called into play the prophecy division of the mind and Raeillo/ee13 and Raellu//2, who had been merely interested onlookers before, hurriedly meshed themselves with the other forty nine hundred odd of their fellows. (It was impossible to say at any given time just how many there were in their computer section, as several births and deaths had occurred among the group since beginning the current observations. These would be suspended for the next several moments, however, as there was a strict prohibition against anyone being born, dying, or otherwise engaging in extraneous activity while their particular bank was either alerted or in action.)

Raeillo/ee13 and Raellu//2 felt the group discipline take hold much more firmly than the free-and-easy mesh which each unit enjoyed with the complete group-mind during periods of leisure.

With a speed that would have been dizzying and incomprehensible to any individual unit, the observing banks relayed huge masses of extraneous data to the interpretive bank. They strained out the salient facts and in turn passed these to the computing:prediction section. Here they were routed to the groups who would deal with them. Raeillo/ee13 and Raellu//2 found their own talents pressed into service a dozen or more times in the space of the minute and a half it took the computing:prediction and interpretive banks to arrive at the answer.

"It's aimed here," the interpretive bank reported.

"Here!" a jumble of incoherent and anarchistic thoughts resounded from many shocked and temporarily out-of-mesh units.

"Order!" came a sharp command from the elite corps of three thousand disciplinary units.

As stillness settled back over the group-mind the speculative bank once more came in. "By here, do you mean *right* here?"

"Approximately," replied the interpretive bank with what would have sounded suspiciously like a chuckle in a human reply. "According to calculations the craft should land within half a mile of our present location."

"Let's go there then and wait for it!" That thought from the now seldom used reservation of impulse.

The speculative bank murmured, "I wonder if there would be any danger. How hot is that exhaust?"

Calculations were rapidly made and the answer arrived at. The Rell prudently decided to remain where they were for the present.

★ ★ ★

Captain Leonard Brown, USAF, hunched over the instruments in the cramped control cabin which, being the only available space in the ship, doubled as living quarters. A larger man would have found the arrangement impossible. Brown, being 5' 2" and weighing 105 pounds found it merely intolerable.

At the moment he was temporarily able to forget his discomfort, however. The many tiny dials and indicators told a story all their own to Brown's trained vision.

"Just another half hour," he whispered to himself. "Just thirty more minutes and I'll land. It may be just a dead planet but I'll still be the first."

There really wasn't a great deal for Brown to do. The ship was self-guided. The Air Force had trusted robot mechanisms more than human reactions.

Thus Brown's entire active contribution to the flight consisted in watching the dials (which recorded everything, so even watching them was unnecessary) and in pressing the button which would cause the ship to start its return journey.

Of course the scientists could have constructed another mechanism to press the button and made it a completely robot ship. But despite their frailties and imperfections, human beings have certain advantages. Humans can talk. Machines may see and detect far more than their human creators but all they can do is record. They can neither interpret nor satisfactorily describe.

Brown was present not only to report a human's reactions to the first Mars flight; he was also along to see that which the machines might miss.

"We've never satisfactorily defined life," one of his instructors had told Brown shortly after he started the three grueling years of training which had been necessary, "so we can't very well build a foolproof machine for detecting it. That's why we've left room for 105 pounds of dead weight."

"Meaning me?"

"Meaning you."

"And I'm your foolproof machine for detecting life?"

"Let's say you're the closest we can come to it at present. We're banking everything on this first trip. It'll be at least eighteen months later before we can get a second ship into space. So it's up to you to get everything you can, especially evidence of life, preferably animal, if possible. With public support it'll be a hell of a lot easier squeezing appropriations out of Congress for the next ship and to get public support we need the biggest possible play in the newspapers. If anything is newsworthy on Mars it should be evidence of life, even plant life."

So here he was, 105 pounds of concentrated knowledge and anticipation, itching with the desire for action and also from more basic causes having to do with two months confinement in a small space with a minimum of water.

"Life is most probable at the poles," the instructor had said. "You won't be able to stay long so we'll try to set you down right at the South Pole. You won't have room to bring back specimens. So keep your eyes open and absorb everything you see. Don't forget anything. What you bring back in your mind weighs nothing."

★ ★ ★

"It's just sitting there," the observing banks reported, "and the red flame has gone out."

"Is it safe now?" enquired the speculative bank.

"In what way?"

"Is it safe to go near that thing?"

"It's very huge," ventured the observing banks unasked. There was a stir of activity which encompassed practically all except the most simple units and which lasted for perhaps five minutes while the speculative bank's last question was processed.

Finally the interpretive bank reluctantly admitted, "We can't arrive at a positive answer. Too many unknown elements are present. We don't know for sure what caused the flame, when it might start again, or what, if anything, is inside."

"But you said it was a work of intelligence. Doesn't that mean Rell would be inside?"

"Not necessarily. They could have constructed the thing to operate itself."

It was just then that the observing banks reported, "It's opening."

The speculative bank quickly responded, "This is an emergency. We must be able to observe from close up. We'll have to approach it."

"The entire mind?" enquired the disciplinary corps.

The speculative bank hesitated. "No, we'll need to split up. One-fifth of us will go, the rest remain here. It's a short distance and we'll still be able to continue in complete contact."

Those who were to go were quickly sorted out and Raeillo/ee13 was quite thrilled to find he and Raellu//2 were included in the scouting party.

The group set off briskly toward their objective but had moved hardly one hundred yards when a vertigo seemed to overtake them. Raeillo/ee13 found himself swimming helplessly in a vortex of darkness and isolation, blanked off from not only the group-mind and his bank but also from Raellu//2. Frantically he grasped for some sort of stasis, but dependence on the group-mind was too ingrained and he was unable to stir his long-dormant powers of sight and education.

Then the isolation cleared to be replaced by a brief impression of chaos with perhaps a tinge of alienness. Another instant of vertigo followed and then everything was normal once more as the comfortable familiar mesh took hold.

"What was that?" Even the speculative bank sounded frightened.

"Sorry." The usually silent meshing bank sounded abashed. "We weren't prepared for that. Some sort of thought wave is issuing from the opening and it disrupted the group mesh till we were able to take it into calculation and rebuild the mesh around it."

"Thought wave? Then there *are* Rell in that thing."

"Do not compute before the mesh is set," the interpretive bank cautioned. "The presence of Rell, while extremely probable, is not yet entirely certain."

Without waiting for a suggestion from elsewhere the disciplinary group ordered the entire mind forward.

Perhaps, in time of stress, dormant qualities tend to emerge, Raeillo/ee13 mused. Certainly everyone, himself included, appeared to be exercising speculative qualities. Not that specialization isn't a marvelous blessing, he hastily added, in case the disciplinary corps might be scanning his bank. But the disciplinary corps itself was as fascinated by the phenomenon ahead as Raeillo/ee13.

Emerging from the infinitely huge upright thing was a mobile being, also infinitely huge. Not that they were the same size. The mobile one was small enough to fit easily through the opening in the lower portion of the larger. But beyond a certain point words lose meaning and infinitely huge was the closest measurement the tiny Rell could find for either the upright pointed thing or the knobby one which had emerged and was quickly identified as the source of the disrupting thought patterns.

★ ★ ★

Leonard Brown was enjoying himself thoroughly. The inside of a space suit can scarcely be termed comfortable but at least you can move around in it and Brown was making the most of this sensation after two months cramped in his tiny cell. He was, in fact, comporting himself much as a three-year-old might have done after a similar release.

But before long he settled down to the serious business of observing and mentally recording everything in sight.

There were none of the mysterious 'canals' in view, which was disappointing; one piece of glamour the publicity boys would necessarily forego until the next trip. The ice cap itself, if such it could be called, was almost equally disappointing. On Earth it would have been dismissed as a mere frost patch, if this section was typical. For a radius of many yards the ground was blasted bare by the action of the exhaust and nowhere in sight did there appear to be more than the flimsiest covering of white over the brown sandy soil.

"Not even lichens," muttered Brown in disgust.

But disgust cannot long stand against the magic of a fresh new planet and Brown continued his avid, though barren, search until hunger forced his return to the ship. He had been able to detect no life and was completely unaware of his close proximity to the planet's dominant species. It had been considered neither practical nor particularly desirable to build a microscope into the space suit. Simplicity and the least possible weight had been the watchwords here as with everything designed to go aboard the ship.

In any case, a microscope would have done Brown little good in trying to detect the submicroscopic beings of the Rell.

★ ★ ★

The Rell, who had somewhat lost their fear of Brown, hastily retreated when they saw him returning to the still awesome ship.

"But are you *sure* he's *completely* self-powered?" the speculative bank queried. "No Rell inside him at all?"

"There are many Rell-like beings in various parts of him," replied the interpretive bank. "Some help digest his food, others are predators, and still others their enemies. But most are too big and clumsy to have developed intelligence, and even the small ones appear completely mindless."

"But where do the thought waves come from? We all felt them."

"It's hard to accept but we are almost forced to conclude they are emanating from the mobile unit itself, or rather from the living part within the cocoon."

"You're positive they aren't the product of some of the Rell-beings inside?"

"Almost positive. The mesh insists not. In fact, it claims this is an un-Rell like type of intelligence, though that appears to be a contradiction in terms. The thought pattern is completely outside our experience. In fact, it is so alien we haven't broken it down yet to the meaning behind it."

"But if the Rell inside are too large to have developed intelligence, how could this gigantic monster in which they live have done so?"

"We cannot yet say. Remember, the theory that intelligence cannot develop in creatures above a certain size is unproven, even though never before challenged. We've watched other races die through failure to adapt to change so apparently it is true of Rell-like creatures on this world. But who can say about organisms on another world or of the unprecedented size of this one? Completely different physical laws may apply."

It was later that afternoon after the Rell had spent much time observing Brown while Brown was busy observing the landscape that the interpretive bank made the triumphant announcement, "We have it! We've broken the thought waves down to their meanings and know what he's thinking. What would you like to know first?"

"Check and see if there are any Rell inside the other thing or on his home world. They might have constructed him."

"Apparently there are none, or at least no intelligent Rell, on his world. We can't guide his mind but the memory bank recorded all the thoughts we've received and some time ago he was thinking of something he termed 'vermin'. Apparently these are sometimes Rell-like creatures, although far larger. He regards them as a great nuisance, but mindless. The big thing, by the way, he calls a 'ship' and it is utterly lifeless. We needn't fear the flame until this creature leaves."

"What about him? What is he like?"

"That's the most exciting part! He thought of his bodily needs once and we glimpsed a concept dealing with his physical construction. It's incredible! His body is composed almost entirely of water. There's enough water in him alone to prolong the life of the Rell many ages. Further, the air in his 'ship' is heavily impregnated with moisture and he even has reserve supplies of water for his needs."

At this, not only Raeillo/ee13, but all except perhaps the most responsible units felt a shiver of primitive longing and perhaps even greed. Not for millennia had there been such a plentitude of water so close!

"Then can't we appropriate at least part of it?" asked the speculative bank.

"Unfortunately both the 'man', as he calls himself, and his 'ship' are sealed so tightly that we could not penetrate either. Worse yet, almost half his time here is already gone. We don't quite understand his purpose here. His thoughts seem to say he is searching for Rell for some unfathomable reason yet he seems to know nothing of the Rell and cannot even detect us."

★ ★ ★

It was the next day when the time was almost all gone that the two big discoveries were made. During a routine check, the mesh came across a thought of the man's return and a visualization of his home world. It was so startling that the interpretive bank was recalled from its effort to try to devise a means through the spacesuit and set at the new problem.

A hasty check of the man's subconscious thoughts revealed the big news. "Do you know," the interpretive bank announced, "not only does this being's home world have a moist atmosphere like that in his ship but two thirds of the surface of his world is *liquid water!*"

Even the speculative bank was silent for a full two seconds after this news. Then a hasty impulse was sent to the disciplinary corps and the entire mind called into action. An extreme emergency upon which the fate of the race hinged called for the utmost effort by even the humblest members of the group.

The Rell worked diligently and many blind alleys were explored, but it was not for some time that anyone thought of enquiring of the not-too-bright feeding bank how they were managing to keep the mind operating at considerably more than normal power with no frost within feeding distance.

"We're taking moisture from the air," was the answer.

"Where is the moisture coming from?" the interpretive bank was asked.

The answer didn't take long. Rapid measurements supplied it. "Some of it is vaporized frost but that wouldn't be enough for our needs. The only other possibility is that moisture must be seeping away from either the man or his ship despite his sureness that they were both airtight and our own investigations which confirmed it."

They had maintained a cautious distance from the ship for the most part despite the interpretive bank's assurance of no immediate danger. But now they swarmed over both it and the spacesuit determined to detect the leak.

They found none.

And now the man was returning to his ship.

"This is the last time," the mesh warned. It was now or never.

For a second there was conflict over control of the circuits to the disciplinary corps which carried with it command of the organism during the emergency. The speculative bank customarily assumed this responsibility, but a slight schism had developed between it and the interpretive bank. The latter's greater age and skill came into play and victory was quickly won.

From the disciplinary corps came the order, "Stay close to the 'man'."

The interpretive bank explained, "He breathes the air so he'll have to get to it some way."

The defeated speculative bank maintained a sulky silence.

Thus it was that the entire mind of the Rell rode into the interior of the ship through the airlock while clustered around Brown.

The Rell had grasped that the man lived and traveled inside his ship and the necessity for it to be airtight. But so different were the two races' needs that the necessity for an airlock and the consequent slight seepage each time it was used had not occurred to even the interpretive bank.

Inside, many Rell, suddenly intoxicated by the heady moisture-laden air, commenced uniting with each other then splitting away, each such union resulting in another unit of Rell, naturally. The interpretive bank again seized control.

"Stop it! Stop it this instant!" it snapped. "Reproduction must be kept to the former minimum for now. That is a firm order."

Reluctantly the process was halted. The interpretive bank explained, "It would not take long for us to use up the entire supply of water if we indulged in uncontrolled reproduction. That might endanger the whole trip."

"What do we do now?" the speculative bank finally asked.

"There is no way of knowing positively whether the man uses this same atmosphere until he returns to his world or not. For our own safety it would seem best, since Rell-like creatures already inhabit him, that we join them. If any place is safe it will be his interior. And there is plenty of moisture within to sustain us. But we must be good parasites," the interpretive bank warned. "Remember, no undue reproduction no matter how many quarts of moisture seem to be going to waste inside this 'man'. He may need it himself and if he does not survive the ship might not complete its trip."

Brown was just emerging from his space suit so the Rell chose his closest available body opening and flowed as a group into his mouth and nostrils.

"Ahchoo!" sneezed Brown, violently evicting half the Rell.

They re-entered a bit more cautiously in order not to irritate the sensitive membrane again.

"Dammit," said Brown, "don't tell me I've caught a cold clear out here on Mars. Hope I didn't pick up any Martian germs."

But he needn't have worried. By the time he reached Earth he was far less germ-ridden, even if considerably more itchy on the exterior, than when he'd left. The

Rell were good at self-defense and a surprising number of mindless but voracious creatures in Brown's interior had been eliminated.

Brown dreaded having to give the news he carried but he needn't have. He was a conquering hero.

So much fuss was made over the first flight to Mars that Congress promptly voted twice the appropriation for the second ship that the Air Force had requested, despite strong opposition from the Navy and headlines which read:

NO LIFE ON MARS

Actually, as it happened, the headlines were one hundred percent correct, but they neglected to mention, chiefly because the headline writers didn't know it, that there were now two races of intelligent life on Earth.

The Terrible Answer

by Arthur G. Hill

They came down to Mars ahead of the rest because Larkin had bought an unfair advantage—a copy of the Primary Report. There were seven of them, all varying in appearance, but with one thing in common; in the eyes of each glowed the greed for Empire. They came down in a flash of orange tail-fire and they looked first at the Martians.

"Green," marveled Evans. "What a queer shade of green."

"Not important," Cleve, the psychologist, replied. "Merely a matter of pigmentation. White, yellow, black, green. It proves only that God loves variety."

"And lord how they grin."

Cleve peered learnedly. "Doesn't indicate a thing. They were born with those grins. They'll die with them."

Of the seven strong men, Larkin exuded the most power. Thus, his role of leader was a natural one. No man would ever stand in front of Larkin. He said, "To hell with color or the shape of their mouths. What we're after lies inside. Come on. Let's set up a camp."

"For the time being," Cleve cautioned, "we must ignore them. Later, when we know what to do, I'll give the nod."

They brought what they needed out of the ship. They brought the plastic tents, broke the small, attached cylinders, and watched the tents bulge up into living quarters. They set up the vapor condenser and it began filling the water tank from the air about them. They plugged a line into the ship and attached it to the tent-line. Immediately the gasses in the plastic tents began to glow and give off both light and heat.

They did many things while the Martians stood silently by with their arms hanging, their splay-feet flat on the ground, their slash-mouths grinning.

The seven sat down to their first meal under the Martian stars and while they ate the rich, delicate foods, they listened to Larkin. "A new empire waiting to be built. A whole planet—virgin—new."

"Not new," Dane, the archeologist, said. "It's older than Earth. It's been worked before."

Larkin waved an impatient hand. "But hardly scratched. It can have risen and fallen a thousand times for all we care. The important thing is the vital ingredient of empire. Is it here? Can it be harnessed? Are we or are we not, on the threshold of wealth, splendor, and progress so great as to take away the breath?"

And as Larkin spoke, all seven men looked at the Martians; looked covertly while appearing to study the rolling plain and the purple ridges far away; the texture of the soil; the color of the sky; the food on their plates. They looked at all these things but they studied the Martians.

"Stupid-looking animals," Evans muttered. "Odd though. So like us, yet so different."

At first there had been only a handful of Martians to grin at the landing of the ship. Now they numbered over a hundred, their ranks augmented by stragglers who came to stare with their fellows in happy silence.

"The prospects are excellent," Cleve said. Then he jerked his attention back to Larkin from whom it had momentarily wandered. When Larkin spoke, one listened.

Larkin had been directing his words toward a young man named Smith. Smith had inherited a great deal of money, which was perfect for helping finance an empire. But Larkin wasn't too sure of his qualifications otherwise. "The pyramids," Larkin was saying. "Would they have ever been built if the men up above, the men with vision, had to worry about a payroll?"

Smith regarded the Martians with not quite the impersonal stare of the other six Earthlings. Once or twice he grinned back at them. "I'll grant the truth of what you say," he told Larkin, "but what good were the pyramids? They're something I could never figure."

Smith had a sardonic twist of mouth that annoyed Larkin. "I merely used the pyramids as an example. Call them a symbol of empire. Every empire on Earth from the beginning of known history built monuments and symbols. Face facts, man."

"Facts?" Smith asked. He had been looking at a six-foot-six Martian, thinking what a magnificent specimen he was. If only they'd wipe off those silly grins.

"Yes, facts," said Larkin, jabbing the table with his finger. "The building must be done. It is a law of nature. Man must progress or not. And what empire can arise without free labor? Can we develop this planet at union scale? Impossible! Yet it's crying to be developed."

Cleve knocked the ashes off his cigar and frowned. Being a man of direct action, he inquired. "Do you want your money back, Smith?"

The latter shook his head. "Oh no! Don't get me wrong, gentlemen. I'm for empire first, last and always. And if we can lay the foundations of one on the backs of these stupid creatures, I'm for it."

"I still don't like your—"

"My outspoken manner?" Smith asked Larkin. "Don't give it a thought, old man. I just don't want to be all cloyed up with platitudes. If we're going to chain the children of Israel into the house of bondage, let's get on with it."

"I don't like your attitude, Smith," Larkin said stubbornly. "In the long run, what we do will benefit these people."

"Let's say, rather, that it may benefit their children. I doubt if these jokers will be around very long after we start cracking the whip."

Dane was stirred. "The whip," he murmured. "Symbol of empire." But nobody heard him. They were too busy listening to Larkin and Smith—and watching the Martians.

The Martians stood around grinning, waiting patiently for something to happen. Larkin's attitude toward them had changed again. First there had been curiosity, then a narrow-eyed calculation; now he regarded them with contempt. The careful, studied checks and tests would be made of course. But Larkin, a man of sure instincts, had already made up his mind.

He stretched luxuriously. "Let's call it a day and turn in. Tomorrow we'll go about the business at hand with clearer heads."

"A good idea," Cleve said, "but first, one little gesture. I think it would be judicious." He eyed the Martians, settling finally upon one—a male—standing close and somewhat apart from the rest. Cleve scowled. Standing erect, he called, "Hey, you!" He interpreted the words with a beckoning gesture of his arm. "Come here! Here, boy! Over here!"

The Martian reacted with a typically Earthian gesture. He pointed to his own chest with one green finger, while a questioning expression reflected through the eternal grin.

"Yes, you! On the double."

The Martian came forward. There was in his manner a slight hesitation, and Smith expected to see his hind quarters wriggle like that of a dog—uncertain, but eager to please.

Cleve pointed with a martinet gesture toward the smoked-out cigar butt he'd thrown to the ground. "Pick it up!"

The Martian stood motionless.

"Pick... it... *up*, you stupid lout!"

The Martian understood. With a glad little whimper, he bent over and took the cigar butt in his hand.

"There," Cleve said. "Garbage can! Get it? *Garbage can*. Place for trash—for cigar butts. Put it in there."

Smith wasn't sure whether the grin deepened or not. He thought it did, as the Martian laid the cigar butt carefully into the trash can.

"Okay, you fella," Cleve barked, still scowling. "Back and away now. Stay out there! Get it? Only come when you're called."

It took a few eloquent gestures, including the pantomime of swinging a whip, before the Martian understood and complied. After he backed into the circle of his fellows, Cleve dropped the cruel overseer manner and turned with satisfaction to Larkin. "I think there will be no trouble at all," he said. "Tomorrow we'll really get down to cases. I predict smooth sailing."

They said goodnight to each other and went about the business of preparing for slumber. As he raised the glowing flap of his tent, Larkin saw Smith lounging in a chair before the electric heat unit. "Aren't you going to get some sleep?"

"In a little while. I'm going to wait around until those two famous moons come. Want to see them first hand."

"A waste of time," Larkin said. "Better keep your mind on more important things."

"Goodnight," Smith said. Larkin did not reply, and Smith turned his head to look at the Martians. He wondered where they had come from. They probably had a village somewhere over the rise. He regarded them without fear or apprehension of what might occur during the sleeping hours. He had read the Primary Report, brought back by the pioneer expedition. These people were entirely harmless. Also they were possessed of remarkable stamina. They had stood for days, watching the first expedition, grinning at it, without nourishment of any kind.

Maybe they live off the atmosphere, Smith told himself dreamily. At any rate, they were ideal specimens to use as the foundation stones of an empire. He lay back, thinking of Larkin. He did not like Larkin personally, but he had to admire the steel in the man, the unswerving determination that had made him what he was.

His mind drifted back to the things of beauty around him. The far purple ridges had changed now, as a light bloomed behind them to gleam like azure through old crystal. Then the two moons shot over the horizon, huge silver bullets riding the thin atmosphere.

The oldest planet. Had it ever been great? Were the bones of any dead civilizations moldering beneath this strange yellow soil? Smith closed his eyes while the cool Martian breezes soothed his face. Greatness. What was greatness after all? Merely a matter of viewpoint perhaps.

Smith got up and moved slowly toward his tent. Out in the shadows he could feel the grins of the Martians. "Goodnight," he called.

But there was no answer.

★ ★ ★

"I put them out there," Cleve said. "It seemed as good a place as any."

"Fine," Larkin rumbled. He wore boots and britches and a big, wide-brimmed hat. He had on soft leather gloves. He looked like an empire builder.

The Martians were standing around grinning at the pile of shovels lying in the fuzz-bush. The Martians seemed interested and appeared to communicate with one another in some imperceptible manner.

Larkin shoved through the circle of green men, pushing rudely. He stopped, picked up one of the shovels; thrust it toward a Martian. The Martian took it in his hands.

"It's very important that you *tell* them—that you don't show them," Cleve said. "You must not do any of the work yourself."

"I'll handle it," Larkin snapped. "Now, you—all of you! Grab a shovel. Pick 'em up, see? Pick 'em up! We've got work to do. A ditch to dig."

Larkin's pantomime was a universal language. "We start the ditch here. Right here. You, fella! Get digging! And put your back into that shovel. Work it hard or maybe your back gets the whip—understand?" Larkin made a threatening motion toward the lash coiled at his belt.

Smith, already on the scene, turned as Evans and Dane arrived carrying undefined plastic. They snapped the cylinders and chairs appeared; chairs—and a table upon which Carter and Lewis, bringing up the rear, placed a pitcher of beer, glasses and a box of cigars.

Cleve, the psychologist, looked with satisfaction upon the string of Martians manipulating the shovels. "All right," he said. "Let's sit down. Pour the beer, one of you."

"Allow me," Smith said. He fought to straighten the smile bending his lips. He picked up the pitcher and poured beer into the glasses. It all seemed so absurd, these grim-faced men acting out an asinine tableau.

Cleve caught the smile. "I wish you'd take this seriously," he said. "It's a mighty touchy and important business."

"Sorry," Smith said, raising his glass. "Here's to empire."

Larkin was striding up and down the line of straining Martians. The scowl had become a part of him.

It's getting him, Smith marveled. *Act or no act, he likes it. Experiment or not, he's in his element.*

The six men sat drinking their beer and watching Larkin. But only Cleve was aware of the skill with which the man worked. The gradual application of pressure; the careful moving forward from bog to bog with the path of retreat always open. From sharpness to brusqueness. From the brusque to the harsh. From the harsh to the brutal.

"Will you tell me," Smith asked, "why we have to sit here drinking like a pack of fools? I don't like beer."

"I'm not enjoying it, either," Cleve said. "But you can certainly understand that the roles must be set right from the beginning. They must understand we are their masters, so we must conduct ourselves in that manner. Never any sign that could be interpreted as compromise."

Larkin, satisfied with the progress of the entirely useless ditch, came to the table and raised a glass of beer. He wiped the foam from his mustache and asked, "What do you think?" directing the question toward Cleve.

The latter regarded the sweating Martians with calculating eyes. "It's going entirely as I predicted. The next step is in order, I believe."

"You think it's safe?"

"I'm certain of it."

Smith, studying Larkin, saw the latter smile, and was again struck by its quality.

Whatever the test, Larkin's for it, even above the call of scientific experimentation.

Larkin was uncoiling the whip from his belt. He strode toward the fast-deepening ditch. He selected a subject. "You, fella! You're lazy, huh? You like to gold-brick it? Then see how you like this!" He laid the whip across the green shoulders of the Martian.

The Martian winced. He raised an arm to shield off the whip. Again it curled against his flesh. He whimpered. His grin was stark, inquiring.

"Hit that shovel, you green bastard!" Larkin roared.

The Martian understood. So did the other Martians. Their muscles quivered as they drove into their work.

Larkin came back, smiling—almost dreamily, Smith thought. Cleve said, "Excellent. I'd hardly hoped for such conformity. Hardly expected it."

"You mean," Smith asked, "that this little scene can be projected from a dozen to a hundred? From a hundred to a thousand?"

"From this little plot to the whole, surface of the planet," Cleve said. "The mass is nothing more than a collection of individuals. Control the individual and you've got the mob. That is if you follow through with the original method. Set the hard pattern."

"Then we're in, is that it? They've passed every test with flying colors."

"I'm sure they will," Cleve said, frowning. "But we must be thorough."

"There's still another test?"

"Yes. The test of final and complete subservience. It must be proven beyond all doubt that they know their masters."

"You don't think they're aware yet that we *are* their masters?"

"I'm sure they know. It only remains to be proven." Cleve glanced up at Larkin. "Maybe this is as far as we should go today. We've made marvelous progress."

That characteristic wave of Larkin's hand; the gesture of the empire builder brushing away mountains. "Why wait? I want to get this thing over with. You said yourself they're under our thumb."

Cleve pondered, staring at the Martians. "Very well. There's really no reason to wait."

Larkin smiled and turned toward the diggers, only half visible now from the depths of the ditch. He walked forward, appearing to exercise more care, this time, in the selection of his subject. Finally, he pointed at one of the Martians. "You! Come here!"

Several of them looked at one another a trifle confused. "You, damn it! What are you waiting for?"

One of them climbed slowly from the trench. While he was engaged in so doing, Smith noticed two things. He saw the look of rage, simulated or otherwise, that came into Larkin's face. And he saw Cleve's fingers tighten on the edge of the table.

Larkin had a gun in his fist; a roar in his voice. "When I talk, you jump! Get that? All of you!"

He fired three bullets into the Martian's brain. The latter slumped grinning to the ground. Larkin, his breath coming jerkily, stood poised on the balls of his feet. The men at the table sat frozen, waiting. Around them, on the plain, some two hundred Martians stood motionless.

The final test, Smith thought. *To prove they're cattle.*

A full minute passed after the echo of the gun faded out. Silence.

And nothing.

The Earthmen picked up their breathing where they'd dropped it. Larkin's breath exploded in savage, triumphant voice. The Martians were his.

"Come on, some of you! Dig a hole and bury that carrion! And if anybody still wonders who's boss around here, let him step forward!"

"They took it!" Cleve whispered. "Glory be, they took it!"

Four Martians climbed grinning from the trench. They faced Larkin and stood as though awaiting instructions.

"Dig there," Larkin said.

They went stolidly to work and Larkin pocketed his gun, making the pocketing a gesture of contempt.

"You see," Cleve said, with the tone of one explaining an abstract problem, "we were at somewhat of a disadvantage because they are incapable of indicating emotion by facial expression. Thus the last test was necessary. If we could have judged the degree of fear previously instilled, that last might not have been necessary."

"Just as well to have a double check nonetheless," Dane said. "Look at them! You'd think nothing out of the ordinary had happened."

Larkin strode back to the table. "Glad we got it over with," he said. "Now we *know*. Cleve can head back for Earth tomorrow. Initial supplies will come to about twenty million, I estimate. The rest of us can stay here and really drive these beggars. Get the foundations dug; get the rock down from the hills."

"A planet in glorious resurrection," said Dane, the poet of the group.

"They've got the grave dug," Cleve observed. "They're waiting for orders."

"Such cattle," Evans muttered.

Larkin strode back to the grave. He pointed. "Him, body into the grave. Snap into it. We've got work to do."

The Martians put the body into the grave.

Then a tall, green man appeared behind Larkin. He put his arms around Larkin's body. Another Martian took the gun from Larkin's pocket.

And they pushed the screaming Earthman down into the grave.

Smith sprang to his feet. "For God's sake!"

"Sit down, you fool!" Cleve hissed. "Do you want to die? We've miscalculated. Something's wrong."

The big Martian was standing on Larkin. The others threw in the soil. Larkin, now beyond sanity, was gibbering like an animal.

Smith sat down. The Earthman presented a frozen tableau. Soon the gibbering could no longer be heard and the big Martian stepped out of the grave.

"Leave everything," Cleve whispered. "Get up very casually and walk back to the ship. Get inside it."

"May God help us," Dane quavered.

"Shut up! Act natural."

They went back and got into the ship while the Martians stood patiently about waiting for something to happen. Their patience was rewarded when the ship arose on a great flaming tail from the surface of the planet.

It was a sight worth waiting for.

The Dope on Mars

by Jack Sharkey

My agent was the one who got me the job of going along to write up the first trip to Mars. He was always getting me things like that—appearances on TV shows, or mentions in writers' magazines. If he didn't sell much of my stuff, at least he sold *me*.

"It'll be the biggest break a writer ever got," he told me, two days before blastoff. "Oh, sure there'll be scientific reports on the trip, but the public doesn't want them; they want the *human* slant on things."

"But, Louie," I said weakly, "I'll probably be locked up for the whole trip. If there are fights or accidents, they won't tell *me* about them."

"Nonsense," said Louie, sipping carefully at a paper cup of scalding coffee. "It'll be just like the public going along vicariously. They'll *identify* with you."

"But, Louie," I said, wiping the dampness from my palms on the knees of my trousers as I sat there, "how'll I go about it? A story? An article? A *you-are-there* type of report? What?"

Louie shrugged. "So keep a diary. It'll be more intimate, like."

"But what if nothing happens?" I insisted hopelessly.

Louie smiled. "So you fake it."

I got up from the chair in his office and stepped to the door. "That's dishonest," I pointed out.

"Creative is the word," Louie said.

So I went on the first trip to Mars. And I kept a diary. This is it. And it is honest. Honest it is.

October 1, 1960

They picked the launching date from the March, 1959, New York *Times*, which stated that this was the most likely time for launching. Trip time is supposed to take 260 days (that's one way), so we're aimed toward where Mars will be (had *better* be, or else).

There are five of us on board. A pilot, co-pilot, navigator and biochemist. And, of course, me. I've met all but the pilot (he's very busy today), and they seem friendly enough.

Dwight Kroger, the biochemist, is rather old to take the "rigors of the journey," as he puts it, but the government had a choice between sending a green scientist who could stand the trip or an accomplished man who would probably not survive, so they picked Kroger. We've blasted off, though, and he's still with us. He looks a damn sight better than I feel. He's kind of balding, and very iron-gray-haired and skinny, but his skin is tan as an Indian's, and right now he's telling jokes in the washroom with the co-pilot.

Jones (that's the co-pilot; I didn't quite catch his first name) is scarlet-faced, barrel-chested and gives the general appearance of belonging under the spreading chestnut tree, not in a metal bullet flinging itself out into airless space. Come to think of it, who *does* belong where we are?

The navigator's name is Lloyd Streeter, but I haven't seen his face yet. He has a little cubicle behind the pilot's compartment, with all kinds of maps and rulers and things. He keeps bent low over a welded-to-the-wall (they call it the bulkhead, for some reason or other) table, scratching away with a ballpoint pen on the maps, and now and then calling numbers over a microphone to the pilot. His hair is red and curly, and he looks as though he'd be tall if he ever gets to stand up. There are freckles on the backs of his hands, so I think he's probably got them on his face, too. So far, all he's said is, "Scram, I'm busy."

Kroger tells me that the pilot's name is Patrick Desmond, but that I can call him Pat when I get to know him better. So far, he's still Captain Desmond to me. I haven't the vaguest idea what he looks like. He was already on board when I got here, so we didn't meet.

My compartment is small but clean. I mean clean now. It wasn't during blastoff. The inertial gravities didn't bother me so much as the gyroscopic spin they put on the ship so we have a sort of artificial gravity to hold us against the curved floor. It's that constant whirly feeling that gets me. I get sick on merry-go-rounds, too.

They're having pork for dinner today. Not me.

October 2, 1960

Feeling much better today. Kroger gave me a box of Dramamine pills. He says they'll help my stomach. So far, so good.

Lloyd came by, also. "You play chess?" he asked.

"A little," I admitted.

"How about a game sometime?"

"Sure," I said. "Do you have a board?"

He didn't.

Lloyd went away then, but the interview wasn't wasted. I learned that he *is* tall and *does* have a freckled face. Maybe we can build a chessboard. With my paper and his ballpoint pen and ruler, it should be easy. Don't know what we'll use for pieces, though.

Jones (I still haven't learned his first name) has been up with the pilot all day. He passed my room on the way to the galley (the kitchen) for a cup of dark brown coffee (they like it thick) and told me that we were almost past the Moon. I asked to look, but he said not yet; the instrument panel is Top Secret. They'd have to cover it so I could look out the viewing screen, and they still need it for steering or something.

I still haven't met the pilot.

October 3, 1960

Well, I've met the pilot. He is kind of squat, with a vulturish neck and close-set jet-black eyes that make him look rather mean, but he was pleasant enough, and said I could call him Pat. I still don't know Jones' first name, though Pat spoke to him, and it sounded like Flants. That can't be right.

Also, I am one of the first five men in the history of the world to see the opposite side of the Moon, with a bluish blurred crescent beyond it that Pat said was the Earth. The back of the Moon isn't much different from the front. As to the space in front of the ship, well, it's all black with white dots in it, and none of the dots move, except in a circle that Pat says is a "torque" result from the gyroscopic spin we're in. Actually, he explained to me, the screen is supposed to keep the image of space locked into place no matter how much we spin. But there's some kind of a "drag." I told him I hoped it didn't mean we'd land on Mars upside down. He just stared at me.

I can't say I was too impressed with that 16 x 19 view of outer space. It's been done much better in the movies. There's just no awesomeness to it, no sense of depth or immensity. It's as impressive as a piece of velvet with salt sprinkled on it.

Lloyd and I made a chessboard out of a carton. Right now we're using buttons for men. He's one of these fast players who don't stop and think out their moves. And so far I haven't won a game.

It looks like a long trip.

October 4, 1960

I won a game. Lloyd mistook my queen-button for my bishop-button and left his king in jeopardy, and I checkmated him next move. He said chess was a waste of time and he had important work to do and he went away.

I went to the galley for coffee and had a talk about moss with Kroger. He said there was a good chance of lichen on Mars, and I misunderstood and said, "A good chance of liking *what* on Mars?" and Kroger finished his coffee and went up front.

When I got back to my compartment, Lloyd had taken away the chessboard and all his buttons. He told me later he needed it to back up a star map.

Pat slept mostly all day in his compartment, and Jones sat and watched the screen revolve. There wasn't much to do, so I wrote a poem, sort of.

Mary, Mary, quite contrary, how does your garden grow? With Martian rime, Venusian slime, and a radioactive hoe.

I showed it to Kroger. He says it may prove to be environmentally accurate, but that I should stick to prose.

October 5, 1960

Learned Jones' first name. He wrote something in the ship's log, and I saw his signature. His name is Fleance, like in "Macbeth." He prefers to be called Jones. Pat uses his first name as a gag. Some fun.

And only 255 days to go.

April 1, 1961

I've skipped over the last 177 days or so, because there's nothing much new. I brought some books with me on the trip, books that I'd always meant to read and never had the time. So now I know all about *Vanity Fair, Pride and Prejudice, War and Peace, Gone with the Wind,* and *Babbitt.*

They didn't take as long as I thought they would, except for *Vanity Fair.* It must have been a riot when it first came out. I mean, all those sly digs at the aristocracy, with copious interpolations by Mr. Thackeray in case you didn't get it when he'd pulled a particularly good gag. Some fun.

And only 78 days to go.

June 1, 1961

Only 17 days to go. I saw Mars on the screen today. It seems to be descending from overhead, but Pat says that that's the "torque" doing it. Actually, it's we who are coming in sideways.

We've all grown beards, too. Pat said it was against regulations, but what the hell. We have a contest. Longest whiskers on landing gets a prize.

I asked Pat what the prize was and he told me to go to hell.

June 18, 1961

Mars has the whole screen filled. Looks like Death Valley. No sign of canals, but Pat says that's because of the dust storm down below. It's nice to have a "down below" again. We're going to land, so I have to go to my bunk. It's all foam rubber, nylon braid supports and magnesium tubing. Might as well be cement for all the good it did me at takeoff. Earth seems awfully far away.

June 19, 1961

Well, we're down. We have to wear gas masks with oxygen hook-ups. Kroger says the air is breathable, but thin, and it has too much dust in it to be any fun to inhale. He's all for going out and looking for lichen, but Pat says he's got to set up camp, then get instructions from Earth. So we just have to wait. The air is very cold, but the Sun is hot as hell when it hits you. The sky is a blinding pink, or maybe more of a pale fuchsia. Kroger says it's the dust. The sand underfoot is kind of rose-colored, and not really gritty. The particles are round and smooth.

No lichen so far. Kroger says maybe in the canals, if there are any canals. Lloyd wants to play chess again.

Jones won the beard contest. Pat gave him a cigar he'd smuggled on board (no smoking was allowed on the ship), and Jones threw it away. He doesn't smoke.

June 20, 1961

Got lost today. Pat told me not to go too far from camp, so, when I took a stroll, I made sure every so often that I could still see the rocket behind me. Walked for maybe an hour; then the oxygen gauge got past the halfway mark, so I started back toward the rocket. After maybe ten steps, the rocket disappeared. One minute it was standing there, tall and silvery, the next instant it was gone.

Turned on my radio pack and got hold of Pat. Told him what happened, and he told Kroger. Kroger said I had been following a mirage, to step back a bit. I did, and I could see the ship again. Kroger said to try and walk toward where the ship seemed to be, even when it wasn't in view, and meantime they'd come out after me in the jeep, following my footprints.

Started walking back, and the ship vanished again. It reappeared, disappeared, but I kept going. Finally saw the real ship, and Lloyd and Jones waving their arms at me. They were shouting through their masks, but I couldn't hear them. The air is too thin to carry sound well.

All at once, something gleamed in their hands, and they started shooting at me with their rifles. That's when I heard the noise behind me. I was too scared to turn around, but finally Jones and Lloyd came running over, and I got up enough nerve to look. There was nothing there, but on the sand, paralleling mine, were footprints. At least I think they were footprints. Twice as long as mine, and three times as wide, but kind of featureless because the sand's loose and dry. They doubled back on themselves, spaced considerably farther apart.

"What was it?" I asked Lloyd when he got to me.

"Damned if I know," he said. "It was red and scaly, and I think it had a tail. It was two heads taller than you." He shuddered. "Ran off when we fired."

"Where," said Jones, "are Pat and Kroger?"

I didn't know. I hadn't seen them, nor the jeep, on my trip back. So we followed the wheel tracks for a while, and they veered off from my trail and followed another, very much like the one that had been paralleling mine when Jones and Lloyd had taken a shot at the scaly thing.

"We'd better get them on the radio," said Jones, turning back toward the ship.

There wasn't anything on the radio but static.

Pat and Kroger haven't come back yet, either.

June 21, 1961

We're not alone here. More of the scaly things have come toward the camp, but a few rifle shots send them away. They hop like kangaroos when they're startled. Their attitudes aren't menacing, but their appearance is. And Jones says, "Who knows what's 'menacing' in an alien?"

We're going to look for Kroger and Pat today. Jones says we'd better before another windstorm blows away the jeep tracks. Fortunately, the jeep has a leaky oil pan, so we always have the smears to follow, unless they get covered up, too. We're taking extra oxygen, shells, and rifles. Food, too, of course. And we're locking up the ship.

★ ★ ★

It's later, now. We found the jeep, but no Kroger or Pat. Lots of those big tracks nearby. We're taking the jeep to follow the aliens' tracks. There's some moss around here, on reddish brown rocks that stick up through the sand, just on the shady side, though. Kroger must be happy to have found his lichen.

The trail ended at the brink of a deep crevice in the ground. Seems to be an earthquake-type split in solid rock, with the sand sifting over this and the far edge like pink silk cataracts. The bottom is in the shade and can't be seen. The crack seems to extend to our left and right as far as we can look.

There looks like a trail down the inside of the crevice, but the Sun's setting, so we're waiting till tomorrow to go down.

Going down was Jones' idea, not mine.

June 22, 1961

Well, we're at the bottom, and there's water here, a shallow stream about thirty feet wide that runs along the center of the canal (we've decided we're in a canal). No sign of Pat or Kroger yet, but the sand here is hard-packed and damp, and there are normal-size footprints mingled with the alien ones, sharp and clear. The aliens seem to have six or seven toes. It varies from print to print. And they're barefoot, too, or else they have the damnedest-looking shoes in creation.

The constant shower of sand near the cliff walls is annoying, but it's sandless (shower-wise) near the stream, so we're following the footprints along the bank. Also, the air's better down here. Still thin, but not as bad as on the surface. We're going without masks to save oxygen for the return trip (Jones assures me there'll *be* a return trip), and the air's only a little bit sandy, but handkerchiefs over nose and mouth solve this.

We look like desperadoes, what with the rifles and covered faces. I said as much to Lloyd and he told me to shut up. Moss all over the cliff walls. Swell luck for Kroger.

★ ★ ★

We've found Kroger and Pat, with the help of the aliens. Or maybe I should call them the Martians. Either way, it's better than what Jones calls them.

They took away our rifles and brought us right to Kroger and Pat, without our even asking. Jones is mad at the way they got the rifles so easily. When we came upon them (a group of maybe ten, huddling behind a boulder in ambush), he fired, but the shots either bounced off their scales or stuck in their thick hides. Anyway, they took the rifles away and threw them into the stream, and picked us all up and took us into a hole in the cliff wall. The hole went on practically forever, but it didn't get dark. Kroger tells me that there are phosphorescent bacteria living in the mold on the walls. The air has a fresh-dug-grave smell, but it's richer in oxygen than even at the stream.

We're in a small cave that is just off a bigger cave where lots of tunnels come together. I can't remember which one we came in through, and neither can anyone else. Jones asked me what the hell I kept writing in the diary for, did I want to make it a gift to Martian archeologists? But I said where there's life there's hope, and now he won't talk to me. I congratulated Kroger on the lichen I'd seen, but he just said a short and unscientific word and went to sleep.

There's a Martian guarding the entrance to our cave. I don't know what they intend to do with us. Feed us, I hope. So far, they've just left us here, and we're out of rations.

Kroger tried talking to the guard once, but he (or it) made a whistling kind of sound and flashed a mouthful of teeth. Kroger says the teeth are in multiple rows, like a tiger shark's. I'd rather he hadn't told me.

June 23, 1961, I think

We're either in a docket or a zoo. I can't tell which. There's a rather square platform surrounded on all four sides by running water, maybe twenty feet across, and we're on it. Martians keep coming to the far edge of the water and looking at us and whistling at each other. A little Martian came near the edge of the water and a larger Martian whistled like crazy and dragged it away.

"Water must be dangerous to them," said Kroger.

"We shoulda brought water pistols," Jones muttered.

Pat said maybe we can swim to safety. Kroger told Pat he was crazy, that the little island we're on here underground is bordered by a fast river that goes into the planet. We'd end up drowned in some grotto in the heart of the planet, says Kroger.

"What the hell," says Pat, "it's better than starving."

It is not.

June 24, 1961, probably

I'm hungry. So is everybody else. Right now I could eat a dinner raw, in a centrifuge, and keep it down. A Martian threw a stone at Jones today, and Jones threw one back at him and broke off a couple of scales. The Martian whistled furiously and went away. When the crowd thinned out, same as it did yesterday (must be some sort of sleeping cycle here), Kroger talked Lloyd into swimming across the river and getting the red scales. Lloyd started at the upstream part of the current, and was about a hundred yards below this underground island before he made the far side. Sure is a swift current.

But he got the scales, walked very far upstream of us, and swam back with them. The stream sides are steep, like in a fjord, and we had to lift him out of the swirling cold water, with the scales gripped in his fist. Or what was left of the scales. They had melted down in the water and left his hand all sticky.

Kroger took the gummy things, studied them in the uncertain light, then tasted them and grinned.

The Martians are made of sugar.

★ ★ ★

Later, same day. Kroger said that the Martian metabolism must be like Terran (Earth-type) metabolism, only with no pancreas to make insulin. They store their energy on the *outside* of their bodies, in the form of scales. He's watched them more closely and seen that they have long rubbery tubes for tongues, and that they now and then suck up water from the stream while they're watching us, being careful not to get their lips (all sugar, of course) wet. He guesses that their "blood" must be almost pure water, and that it washes away (from the inside, of course) the sugar they need for energy.

I asked him where the sugar came from, and he said probably their bodies isolated carbon from something (he thought it might be the moss) and combined it with the hydrogen and oxygen in the water (even *I* knew the formula for water) to make sugar, a common carbohydrate.

Like plants, on Earth, he said. Except, instead of using special cells on leaves to form carbohydrates with the help of sun power, as Earth plants do in photosynthesis (Kroger spelled that word for me), they used the *shape* of the scales like prisms, to isolate the spectra (another Kroger word) necessary to form the sugar.

"I don't get it," I said politely, when he'd finished his spiel.

"Simple," he said, as though he were addressing me by name. "They have a twofold reason to fear water. One: by complete solvency in that medium, they lose all energy and die. Two: even partial sprinkling alters the shape of the scales, and they are unable to use sun power to form more sugar, and still die, if a bit slower."

"Oh," I said, taking it down verbatim. "So now what do we do?"

"We remove our boots," said Kroger, sitting on the ground and doing so, "and then we cross this stream, fill the boots with water, and *spray* our way to freedom."

"Which tunnel do we take?" asked Pat, his eyes aglow at the thought of escape.

Kroger shrugged. "We'll have to chance taking any that seem to slope upward. In any event, we can always follow it back and start again."

"I dunno," said Jones. "Remember those *teeth* of theirs. They must be for biting something more substantial than moss, Kroger."

"We'll risk it," said Pat. "It's better to go down fighting than to die of starvation."

The hell it is.

37

June 24, 1961, for sure

The Martians have coal mines. *That's* what they use those teeth for. We passed through one and surprised a lot of them chewing gritty hunks of anthracite out of the walls. They came running at us, whistling with those tube-like tongues, and drooling dry coal dust, but Pat swung one of his boots in an arc that splashed all over the ground in front of them, and they turned tail (literally) and clattered off down another tunnel, sounding like a locomotive whistle gone berserk.

We made the surface in another hour, back in the canal, and were lucky enough to find our own trail to follow toward the place above which the jeep still waited.

Jones got the rifles out of the stream (the Martians had probably thought they were beyond recovery there) and we found the jeep. It was nearly buried in sand, but we got it cleaned off and running, and got back to the ship quickly. First thing we did on arriving was to break out the stores and have a celebration feast just outside the door of the ship.

It was pork again, and I got sick.

June 25, 1961

We're going back. Pat says that a week is all we were allowed to stay and that it's urgent to return and tell what we've learned about Mars (we know there are Martians, and they're made of sugar).

"Why," I said, "can't we just tell it on the radio?"

"Because," said Pat, "if we tell them now, by the time we get back we'll be yesterday's news. This way we may be lucky and get a parade."

"Maybe even money," said Kroger, whose mind wasn't always on science.

"But they'll ask why we didn't radio the info, sir," said Jones uneasily.

"The radio," said Pat, nodding to Lloyd, "was unfortunately broken shortly after landing."

Lloyd blinked, then nodded back and walked around the rocket. I heard a crunching sound and the shattering of glass, not unlike the noise made when one drives a rifle butt through a radio.

Well, it's time for takeoff.

★ ★ ★

This time it wasn't so bad. I thought I was getting my space-legs, but Pat says there's less gravity on Mars, so escape velocity didn't have to be so fast, hence a smoother (relatively) trip on our shock-absorbing bunks.

Lloyd wants to play chess again. I'll be careful not to win this time. However, if I don't win, maybe this time *I'll* be the one to quit.

Kroger is busy in his cramped lab space trying to classify the little moss he was able to gather, and Jones and Pat are up front watching the white specks revolve on that black velvet again.

Guess I'll take a nap.

June 26, 1961

Hell's bells. Kroger says there are two baby Martians loose on board ship. Pat told him he was nuts, but there are certain signs he's right. Like the missing charcoal in the air-filtration-and-reclaiming (AFAR) system. And the water gauges are going down. But the clincher is those two sugar crystals Lloyd had grabbed up when we were in that zoo. They're gone.

Pat has declared a state of emergency. Quick thinking, that's Pat. Lloyd, before he remembered and turned scarlet, suggested we radio Earth for instructions. We can't.

Here we are, somewhere in a void headed for Earth, with enough air and water left for maybe three days—if the Martians don't take any more.

Kroger is thrilled that he is learning something, maybe, about Martian reproductive processes. When he told Pat, Pat put it to a vote whether or not to jettison Kroger through the airlock. However, it was decided that responsibility was pretty well divided. Lloyd had gotten the crystals, Kroger had only studied them, and Jones had brought them aboard.

So Kroger stays, but meanwhile the air is getting worse. Pat suggested Kroger put us all into a state of suspended animation till landing time, eight months away. Kroger said, "How?"

June 27, 1961

Air is foul and I'm very thirsty. Kroger says that at least—when the Martians get bigger—they'll have to show themselves. Pat says what do we do *then*? We can't afford the water we need to melt them down. Besides, the melted crystals might *all* turn into little Martians.

Jones says he'll go down spitting.

Pat says why not dismantle interior of rocket to find out where they're holing up? Fine idea.

How do you dismantle riveted metal plates?

June 28, 1961

The AFAR system is no more and the water gauges are still dropping. Kroger suggests baking bread, then slicing it, then toasting it till it turns to carbon, and we can use the carbon in the AFAR system.

We'll have to try it, I guess.

The Martians ate the bread. Jones came forward to tell us the loaves were cooling, and when he got back they were gone. However, he did find a few of the red crystals on the galley deck (floor). They're good-sized crystals, too. Which means so are the Martians.

Kroger says the Martians must be intelligent, otherwise they couldn't have guessed at the carbohydrates present in the bread after a lifelong diet of anthracite. Pat says let's jettison Kroger.

This time the vote went against Kroger, but he got a last-minute reprieve by suggesting the crystals be pulverized and mixed with sulfuric acid. He says this'll produce carbon.

I certainly hope so.

So does Kroger.

★ ★ ★

Brief reprieve for us. The acid-sugar combination not only produces carbon but water vapor, and the gauge has gone up a notch. That means that we have a quart of water in the tanks for drinking. However, the air's a bit better, and we voted to let Kroger stay inside the rocket.

Meantime, we have to catch those Martians.

June 29, 1961

Worse and worse. Lloyd caught one of the Martians in the firing chamber. We had to flood the chamber with acid to subdue the creature, which carbonized nicely. So now we have plenty of air and water again, but besides having another Martian still on the loose, we now don't have enough acid left in the fuel tanks to make a landing.

Pat says at least our vector will carry us to Earth and we can die on our home planet, which is better than perishing in space.

The hell it is.

March 3, 1962

Earth in sight. The other Martian is still with us. He's where we can't get at him without blow-torches, but he can't get at the carbon in the AFAR system, either, which is a help. However, his tail is prehensile, and now and then it snakes out through an air duct and yanks food right off the table from under our noses.

Kroger says watch out. *We* are made of carbohydrates, too. I'd rather not have known.

March 4, 1962

Earth fills the screen in the control room. Pat says if we're lucky, he might be able to use the bit of fuel we have left to set us in a descending spiral into one of the oceans. The rocket is tighter than a submarine, he insists, and it will float till we're rescued, if the plates don't crack under the impact.

We all agreed to try it. Not that we thought it had a good chance of working, but none of us had a better idea.

★ ★ ★

I guess you know the rest of the story, about how that destroyer spotted us and got us and my diary aboard, and towed the rocket to San Francisco. News of the "captured Martian" leaked out, and we all became nine-day wonders until the dismantling of the rocket.

Kroger says he must have dissolved in the water, and wonders what *that* would do. There are about a thousand of those crystal-scales on a Martian.

So last week we found out, when those red-scaled things began clambering out of the sea on every coastal region on Earth. Kroger tried to explain to me about salinity osmosis and hydrostatic pressure and crystalline life, but in no time at all he lost me.

The point is, bullets won't stop these things, and wherever a crystal falls, a new Martian springs up in a few weeks. It looks like the five of us have abetted an invasion from Mars.

Needless to say, we're no longer heroes.

I haven't heard from Pat or Lloyd for a week. Jones was picked up attacking a candy factory yesterday, and Kroger and I were allowed to sign on for the flight to Venus scheduled within the next few days—because of our experience.

Kroger says there's only enough fuel for a one-way trip. I don't care. I've always wanted to travel with the President.

I Like Martian Music

by Charles E. Fritch

Longtree sat before his hole in the ground and gazed thoughtfully among the sandy red hills that surrounded him. His skin at that moment was a medium yellow, a shade between pride and happiness at having his brief symphony almost completed, with just a faint tinge of red denoting an uncertain, cautious approach to the last note which had eluded him thus far.

He sat there unmoving for a while, and then he picked up his blowstring and fitted the mouthpiece between his thin lips. He blew into it softly and at the same time gently strummed the three strings stretching the length of the instrument. The note rose firm and clear, which would have made any other musician proud.

But Longtree frowned. His body flushed dark green with disappointment and began taking on a purple cast of anger. Hastily, he put down the blowstring and tried to think of something else. Slowly his normal color returned.

Across the nearest hill came his friend Channeljumper, striding on the long, ungainly legs that had given him his name. His skin radiated a blissful orange.

"Longtree!" Channeljumper exclaimed enthusiastically, collapsing on the ground nearby and folding his legs around him. "How's the symphony coming?"

"Not so good," Longtree admitted sadly, and his skin turned green at the memory. "If I don't get that last note, I may be this color the rest of my life."

"Why don't you play what you've written so far? It's not very long, and it might cheer you up a bit."

You're a good friend, Channeljumper, Longtree thought, *and when Redsand and I are married after the Music Festival we'll have you over to our hole for dinner.* As he thought this, he felt his body take on an orange cast, and he felt better.

"I can't seem to get that last note," he said, picking up the blowstring again and putting it into position. "The final note must be conclusive, something complete in itself and yet be able to sum up the entire meaning of the symphony preceding it."

Channeljumper hummed sympathetically. "That's a big job for one note. It might be a sound no one has ever heard before."

Longtree shrugged. "It may even sound alien," he admitted, "but it's got to be the right note."

"Play, and we'll see," Channeljumper urged.

Longtree played. And as he played, his features relaxed into a gentle smile of happiness and his body turned orange. Delicately, he strummed the three strings of the blowstring with his long-nailed fingers, softly he pursed his frail lips and blew expertly into the mouthpiece.

From the instrument came sounds the like of which Channeljumper had never before heard. The Martian sat and listened in rapture, his body radiating a golden glow of ecstasy. He sat and dreamed, and as the music played, his spine tingled with growing excitement. The music swelled, surrounding him, permeating him, picking him up in a great hand and sweeping him into new and strange and beautiful worlds—worlds of tall metal structures, of vast stretches of greenness and of water and of trees and of small pale creatures that flew on the backs of giant metal insects. He dreamed of these things which his planet Mars had not known for millions of years.

After a while, the music stopped, but for a moment neither of them said anything.

At last Channeljumper sighed. "It's beautiful," he said.

"Yes," Longtree admitted.

"But..." Channeljumper seemed puzzled. "But somehow it doesn't seem complete. Almost, but not quite. As though..."

Longtree sighed. "One more note would do it. One more note—no more, no less—at the end of the crescendo could tie the symphony together and end it. But which one? I've tried them all, and none of them fit."

His voice had risen higher in his excitement, and Channeljumper warned, "Careful, you're beginning to turn purple."

"I know," Longtree said mournfully, and the purple tint changed to a more acceptable green. "But I've got to win first prize at the festival tomorrow; Redsand promised to marry me if I did."

"You can't lose," Channeljumper told him, and then remembered, "if you can get that last note."

"If," Longtree echoed despairingly, as though his friend had asked the impossible. "I wish I had your confidence, Chan. You're orange most of the time, while I'm a spectrum."

"I haven't your artistic temperament," Channeljumper told him. "Besides, orange is such a homely color I feel ashamed to have it all the time."

As he said this, he turned light green with shame, and Longtree laughed at the paradox.

Channeljumper laughed too, glad that he had diverted his friend's attention from the elusive and perhaps non-existent note. "Did you know the space rocket is due pretty soon," he said, "perhaps even in time for the Music Festival?"

"Space rocket?"

"Oh, I forgot you were busy composing and didn't get to hear about it," Channeljumper said. "Well, Bigwind, who has a telescope in his hole, told me a rocket is coming through space toward us, possibly from the third planet."

"Oh?" Longtree said, not particularly interested.

"Do you think they will look like us?" Channeljumper wondered.

"If they're intelligent, of course they will," Longtree said with certainty, not caring. "Their culture will probably be alien, though, and their music—" He paused and turned a very deep yellow. "Of course! They might even be able to furnish the note I need to complete my symphony!"

Channeljumper shook his head. "You've got to compose it all yourself," he reminded, "or you don't qualify. And if you don't qualify, you can't win, and if you don't win, you can't marry Redsand."

"But it is just one little note." Longtree said.

Channeljumper shrugged helplessly and turned sympathetically brown. "I don't make the rules," he said.

"No. Well," Longtree went on in sudden determination, "I'll find that last note if I have to stay permanently purple."

Channeljumper shuddered jestingly at this but remained pleasantly orange. "And I'll leave you alone so you can get to work," he said, unfolding himself.

"Goodbye," Longtree said, but Channeljumper's long legs had already taken him over to the nearest sand dune and out of sight.

Alone, Longtree picked up the blowstring once more, placed his lips on the mouthpiece, and produced a clear, beautiful, experimental note, which was again not the one he desired.

He still had not found it an hour later, when the sound came. The sound was a low unpleasant rumble, a sound lower than any Longtree had ever heard, and he wondered what it was. Thinking of it, he remembered he had seen a large flash of fire in the sky a moment before the roar came. But since this last was clearly not likely at all, he dismissed the whole thing as imagination and tried again to coax some new note from the blowstring.

A half hour later, Channeljumper came bounding excitedly over a sand dune. "They're here," he cried, screeching to a halt and emitting yellow flashes of color.

"Who's here?" Longtree demanded, turning violet in annoyance at the interruption.

"The visitors from space," Channeljumper explained. "They landed near my hole. They're little creatures, only half as big as we are, but thicker and grey colored."

"Grey colored?" Longtree repeated incredulously, trying to picture the improbability.

"But only on the outside," Channeljumper went on. "They have an outside shell that comes off, and inside they're sort of pink-orange."

"Ah-ha," Longtree said, as though he'd suspected it all the time. "Evidently they wear grey suits of some kind, probably for protection."

"They took them off anyway," Channeljumper said, eager to impart his knowledge, "and they were sort of pink-orange underneath. There are only two of them, and one has long hair."

"Strange," Longtree mused, thinking of their own hairless bodies. "Wonder what they want."

Channeljumper shrugged to indicate he didn't know. "The short-haired one followed me," he said.

Longtree felt the chill blue of fear creep along his spine, but immediate anger at himself changed it conveniently to purple, and he was certain Channeljumper hadn't noticed. When he had controlled himself, he said, "Well, it doesn't matter. I've got to get on with my symphony. That last note—"

"He's here," Channeljumper announced.

"What?"

Channeljumper pointed eagerly, and Longtree's eyes followed the direction to where the alien stood at the top of a nearby dune staring at them. Longtree could feel his skin automatically turning red with caution, blending with the sand while the ever-trusting Channeljumper remained bright orange.

"Good gosh," the alien exclaimed. "Not only do they look like modified grasshoppers, they change color too!"

"What'd he say?" Longtree demanded.

"How should I know?" Channeljumper said. "It's in another language."

"And its voice," Longtree exclaimed, almost disbelieving it. "Low. Lower than even our drums' rumble."

"And they talk in squeaks!" the alien told himself aloud.

Longtree regarded the alien carefully. As Channeljumper had said, the creature was short and had close-cropped hair on its head. The legs were brief and pudgy, and Longtree felt a shade of pity for the creature who could obviously not get around as well as they. It was undoubtedly intelligent—the space rocket testified to that—and the fact that the creature's skin color stayed a peaceful pink-orange helped assure Longtree the alien's mission was friendly.

The alien raised a short arm and stepped slowly forward. "I come in peace," he said in the language they could not understand. "My wife and I are probably the only humans left alive. When we left Earth, most of the population had been wiped out by atomics. I think we were the only ones to get away."

Longtree felt his redness subside to orange, as he wondered idly what the alien had said. Except for a natural curiosity, he didn't really care, for he remembered suddenly the symphony he had to finish by tomorrow if he were to marry Redsand. But there was the element of politeness to consider, so he nudged Channeljumper.

"Don't just stand there, say something."

Channeljumper flustered and turned several colors in rapid succession. He stammered, "Er—ah—welcome to our planet, O visitor from space," and motioned the alien to sit down.

"That's not very creative," Longtree accused.

"What's the difference," Channeljumper pointed out, "when he doesn't understand us anyway."

"You guys don't really look like grasshoppers," the man from Earth apologized, coming forward; "it's just the long legs that fooled me from up there. Boy, am I glad to find somebody intelligent on Mars; from the air we couldn't see any cities or anything, and we were afraid the planet didn't have any life. I wish we could understand each other, though."

Longtree smiled pleasantly and wished the creature would go away so he could search for the last note to his symphony. He picked up his blowstring so the alien wouldn't sit on it.

"Play for him," Channeljumper suggested, seating himself by segments. "Just the last part to see how he reacts. Music is universal, you know."

Longtree was going to do just that thing, for despite Channeljumper's warning that he must compose every single note by himself, he felt an alien viewpoint might be helpful.

He started playing. Channeljumper sat dreaming, glowing radiantly, but the alien seemed somewhat perturbed by the music and fidgeted nervously. Could it be,

Longtree wondered, that the incredible beauty of his composition might not translate acceptably to alien ears? He dismissed the thought as unlikely.

"That's a bit high, isn't it?" the creature said, shaking his head.

Lost in the sweeping melodies, neither Longtree nor Channeljumper paid any attention to the meaningless syllables. Longtree played on, oblivious to all else, soaring toward the great screaming crescendo that would culminate with the missing note.

Vaguely, he became aware that the creature had gotten up, and he turned a small part of his attention to the action. Longtree smiled inwardly, pleased, and turned yellow with pride to think even a man from another planet should so appreciate his symphony that he got up and danced a strange dance and even sang to the music.

The alien held onto his ears and leaped erratically, singing, "No, no, stop it. It's too high. My head's bursting!"

Channeljumper too seemed pleased by this show of appreciation, though neither of them understood the words, and Longtree swept into the final notes of the rising crescendo with a gusto he had not previously displayed. He stopped where he had always stopped—and the final note came!

It startled the Martians. Then the realization swept over them in glad tides of color. The symphony was complete now, with that final alien sound. Longtree could win both the festival prize and Redsand with it. The last note was a soft popping sound that had come from the creature from another planet. They looked to see him sagging to the ground, his head soft and pulpy.

"My symphony's complete," Longtree exclaimed jubilantly, a brilliant yellow now.

But Channeljumper's yellow happiness was tinged with green. "A pity," he said, "the creature had to give its life in exchange for the note."

"I believe it really wanted to," Longtree said, turning solemn. "Did you see how it danced to the music, in ecstasy, and it didn't change color once! It must have died happy to know it gave itself to a good cause."

"You could probably get by with claiming to use the creature as an auxiliary instrument," mused Channeljumper, practical once more, "and eliminate any claim that he might have assisted you. But what about the Festival? This one looks as though he doesn't have another note in him."

"There's the other one," Longtree reminded, "the one with long hair. We can save that one until tomorrow."

"Of course," Channeljumper agreed, standing up. "I'll go get it, and you can keep it safe here in your hole until tomorrow night."

"You're a good friend, Channeljumper," Longtree began, but the other was already bounding out of sight over a sand dune.

Blissfully he raised the blowstring into position and played the opening notes to his symphony. The alien lay unmoving with its head in a sticky puddle, but Longtree took no notice. He didn't even consider that after the Festival he would never be able to play his symphony again in all its glorious completeness. His spinal column tingled pleasantly, and his skin turned the golden yellow of unbearable happiness.

The music was beautiful.

THE MARTIANS

Keep Out

by Frederic Brown

Daptine is the secret of it. Adaptine, they called it first; then it got shortened to daptine. It let us adapt.

They explained it all to us when we were ten years old. I guess they thought we were too young to understand before then, although we knew a lot of it already. They told us just after we landed on Mars.

"You're *home*, children," the Head Teacher told us after we had gone into the glassite dome they'd built for us there. And he told us there'd be a special lecture for us that evening, an important one that we must all attend.

And that evening he told us the whole story and the whys and wherefores. He stood up before us. He had to wear a heated space suit and helmet, of course, because the temperature in the dome was comfortable for us but already freezing cold for him and the air was already too thin for him to breathe. His voice came to us by radio from inside his helmet.

"Children," he said, "you are home. This is Mars, the planet on which you will spend the rest of your lives. You are Martians, the first Martians. You have lived five years on Earth and another five in space. Now you will spend ten years, until you are adults, in this dome, although toward the end of that time you will be allowed to spend increasingly long periods outdoors.

"Then you will go forth and make your own homes, live your own lives, as Martians. You will intermarry and your children will breed true. They too will be Martians.

"It is time you were told the history of this great experiment of which each of you is a part."

Then he told us.

Man, he said, had first reached Mars in 1985. It had been uninhabited by intelligent life (there is plenty of plant life and a few varieties of non-flying insects) and he had found it by terrestrial standards uninhabitable. Man could survive on Mars only by living inside glassite domes and wearing space suits when he went outside of them. Except by day in the warmer seasons it was too cold for him. The air was too thin for him to breathe and long exposure to sunlight—less filtered of rays harmful to him than on Earth because of the lesser atmosphere—could kill him. The plants were chemically alien to him and he could not eat them; he had to bring all his food from Earth or grow it in hydroponic tanks.

For fifty years he had tried to colonize Mars and all his efforts had failed. Besides this dome which had been built for us there was only one other outpost, another glassite dome much smaller and less than a mile away.

It had looked as though mankind could never spread to the other planets of the solar system besides Earth, for of all of them Mars was the least inhospitable; if he couldn't live here there was no use even trying to colonize the others.

And then, in 2034, thirty years ago, a brilliant biochemist named Waymoth had discovered daptine. A miracle drug that worked not on the animal or person to whom it was given, but on the progeny he conceived during a limited period of time after inoculation.

It gave his progeny almost limitless adaptability to changing conditions, provided the changes were made gradually.

Dr. Waymoth had inoculated and then mated a pair of guinea pigs; they had borne a litter of five and by placing each member of the litter under different and gradually changing conditions, he had obtained amazing results. When they attained maturity one of those guinea pigs was living comfortably at a temperature of forty below zero Fahrenheit, another was quite happy at a hundred and fifty above. A third was thriving on a diet that would have been deadly poison for an ordinary animal and a fourth was contented under a constant X-ray bombardment that would have killed one of its parents within minutes.

Subsequent experiments with many litters showed that animals who had been adapted to similar conditions bred true and their progeny was conditioned from birth to live under those conditions.

"Ten years later, ten years ago," the Head Teacher told us, "you children were born. Born of parents carefully selected from those who volunteered for the experiment. And from birth you have been brought up under carefully controlled and gradually changing conditions.

"From the time you were born the air you have breathed has been very gradually thinned and its oxygen content reduced. Your lungs have compensated by becoming much greater in capacity, which is why your chests are so much larger than those of your teachers and attendants; when you are fully mature and are breathing air like that of Mars, the difference will be even greater.

"Your bodies are growing fur to enable you to stand the increasing cold. You are comfortable now under conditions which would kill ordinary people quickly. Since you were four years old your nurses and teachers have had to wear special protection to survive conditions that seem normal to you.

"In another ten years, at maturity, you will be completely acclimated to Mars. Its air will be your air; its food plants your food. Its extremes of temperature will be easy for you to endure and its median temperatures pleasant to you. Already, because of the five years we spent in space under gradually decreased gravitational pull, the gravity of Mars seems normal to you.

"It will be your planet, to live on and to populate. You are the children of Earth but you are the first Martians."

Of course we had known a lot of those things already.

★ ★ ★

The last year was the best. By then the air inside the dome—except for the pressurized parts where our teachers and attendants live—was almost like that outside, and we were allowed out for increasingly long periods. It is good to be in the open.

The last few months they relaxed segregation of the sexes so we could begin choosing mates, although they told us there is to be no marriage until after the final day, after our full clearance. Choosing was not difficult in my case. I had made my choice long since and I'd felt sure that she felt the same way; I was right.

Tomorrow is the day of our freedom. Tomorrow we will be Martians, *the* Martians. Tomorrow we shall take over the planet.

Some among us are impatient, have been impatient for weeks now, but wiser counsel prevailed and we are waiting. We have waited twenty years and we can wait until the final day.

And tomorrow is the final day.

Tomorrow, at a signal, we will kill the teachers and the other Earthmen among us before we go forth. They do not suspect, so it will be easy.

We have dissimulated for years now, and they do not know how we hate them. They do not know how disgusting and hideous we find them, with their ugly misshapen bodies, so narrow-shouldered and tiny-chested, their weak sibilant voices that need amplification to carry in our Martian air, and above all their hairless skins.

We shall kill them and then we shall go and smash the other dome so all the Earthmen there will die too.

If more Earthmen ever come to punish us, we can live and hide in the hills where they'll never find us. And if they try to build more domes here we'll smash them. We want no more to do with Earth.

This is our planet and we want no aliens. Keep out!

She Knew He Was Coming

by Kris Neville

Outside, the bluish sun slanted low across the green dust of the Martian desert, its last rays sparkling on the far mountain tops. One by one, lights flickered on in the city.

"Mary must be expecting that Earthman," Anne said. She held her glastic blouse tight together over her breasts and leaned a little out of the window.

Milly nodded. "The *Azmuth* landed this morning."

The noises of commerce were fading. From the window Anne saw the neon blaze up over the door. For the thousandth time she blinked between the equivocal words:

30—BEAUTIFUL HOSTESSES—30

Laughter, dry and false, filtered up from the tea bars along the street. She looked westward, toward the spaceport, and made out the shadowy nose of the berthed space liner looming against the night. She could picture the scene—a thousand stevedores unloading cargo, refill men and native spacewriters scurrying over the sleek hull, the Earth voyageurs shouting orders and curses.

"Maybe he isn't even on it." Anne turned from the window. She crossed to the couch and sat down, fluffing out the green crinkly glass of her skirt. Pendant, multicolored birds flashed from the rings in her ears. She tucked rosy feet under her scented body. "I don't like Earthmen," she said.

"They spend money."

"They make me sick," Anne said. "With their pale skins and ugly eyes and hairy bodies."

"They have strong arms."

Anne's wide, red mouth curled in distaste. "They're like a bunch of kids."

The room was lighted by soft, overhead fire. Heavy drapes hung from the walls. Sweet, spicy incense curled bluely from the burners by the window.

Before the mirror, Milly edged in the narrow line of her pink eyebrows with a pencil. She folded her lips in, rubbing them together, licked them, making them a glistening red.

"I wonder when they'll catch Crescent?" she said.

Anne yawned languorously. "It won't be long."

"I wouldn't want to be in her shoes," Milly said.

Anne patted her mouth lazily. "She ought to have known she couldn't run away."

"What do you think Miss Bestris will do to her?"

Anne stood up, brushing out the wrinkles in her dress. "As if I should care."

"But what will she do?"

Anne shrugged. "Whip her, maybe. How should *I* know?"

"Don't you feel you'd like to run away, once in a while?" Milly asked, turning to look at the other girl.

Anne laughed coldly. "I've got better sense."

"But don't you *want* to?"

Anne tossed her purple hair. "Where is there to go? Who is there to go to?"

"Yes, I guess you're right." Milly turned back to her reflection.

Buzzzzzz.

Both girls turned their heads to the buttons on the wall. The white one was glowing.

"It's Miss Bestris."

"We'd better go," Milly said.

Together they walked down the heavily carpeted stairs to the sitting room.

The Madame was waiting. She was a large woman, rolling in creases of fat, and her pink hair was rough and clipped short. She had a pair of dimples in her cheeks and a single gold band around her right wrist. She was leaning against the piano.

"Hurry now, girls, hurry right along," she said.

More girls were entering the room; they spread out, sitting on the chairs, curling at the Madame's feet. Their eyes—amethyst, gray or golden—were on her face. Many had pink hair, others had tresses of purple or salmon.

"Now, girls, I suppose you know there's an Earth ship in port?"

The girls nodded.

"So I expect we'll have visitors tonight. I want you to all look your very best." She smiled at them. "Anne, why don't you wear that low-cut, orange plastic with the spangles, and June, you the prim white one? You look like an angel in it." June smiled. "And Mary...?"

"Yes, Miss Bestris?"

"Mary. Did you buy that neo-nylon I told you about?"

"No, Miss Bestris."

"Mary, Mary, Mary. I just don't understand you at all."

"I'm saving my money, Miss Bestris," Mary said intently.

"Yes, dear, I know that. We're *all* saving our money. But we simply must look presentable. We have a reputation to hold up."

"Yes, Miss Bestris."

"Then, Mary, dear, do—do, *please*, buy yourself something decent."

"Yes, Miss Bestris. I will. Tomorrow. Tomorrow morning, if I ..."

"Child? If you what?"

"Nothing, Miss Bestris."

"Well. See that you get it tomorrow. If you don't, I'm afraid I'll have to take some of your money and get it for you."

Mary looked down at the floor. The flaming glow of the hydrojet torches cast golden lights in her softly purple hair.

"By the way, Mary. Is that your cake in the oven?"

"Yes, Miss Bestris."

The other girls snickered.

"Let her alone," said the Madame. "If she wants to bake a cake, why shouldn't she?"

No one answered.

Miss Bestris went on around the room, discussing the girls' clothing, brushing this girl's hair, pinching that girl's cheek, chucking this one under the chin, smiling, frowning. Then finally she stepped back and nodded.

"You all look quite good, I think. I can be proud of you. And now, I want you all to go to your rooms and make them extra attractive, and then try to get a little rest, so you'll all be especially beautiful when the boys come. Run along now."

The girls filed out, and night continued to settle. After a while, her cigarette glowing in the gloom, the Madame waddled to her office. There three people were waiting for her.

★ ★ ★

The office was plain, businesslike, masculine; no lace, no ribbons, no perfume, only the crisp smell of new paper, the tangy odor of ink, the sweet smell of eraser fluid. When she came in the door the three people stood up.

She waved her cigarette hand with a once delicate gesture and flame light glinted dully on the gold band. "Please don't get up for me," she said, but her tone was condescending and the three visitors sat down respectfully.

Miss Bestris crossed to her desk; she perched on a corner of it, leaned back, blew smoke.

"You wanted to see me about your girls?"

Two of the people, man and wife, looked at each other. "Yes," they said. And the other man said, "Yes."

"Did you bring any pictures?"

They handed her pictures, and she held them up to the overhead torch. She studied them critically, pursing and unpursing her lips in secret calculation.

"This one," she said finally, holding out one of the pictures.

The man and wife rustled their clothing; they smiled faintly proud at each other.

The other man got up slowly, retrieved his picture, left the room without saying a word.

"We can't do for little Lavada," the woman whined. "She was a late child, and we're getting old, and we thought she would be better here. It's hard to do for a growing girl when you get old. And my husband can't keep steady work, because of his health and ..."

"I'm sure she will be happy here," the Madame said, smiling.

"Yes," the man agreed. "It's for the best. But—you know—well, we hate to do it."

"How old is she?"

"Fourteen."

Miss Bestris studied the picture again. "She doesn't look over twelve."

"She's fourteen."

"And healthy."

"We have doctors to see to that," the Madame said. "How much did you have in mind?"

"Well," the man said, "it's been a month now since I worked, and with debts and everything...."

"And something to put aside for winter," his wife added.

"We couldn't take less than a *milli dordoc.*"

"And we wouldn't even think of it, but we don't have a scrap of bread in the house."

"And all our bills, and winter coming on...."

Miss Bestris turned the picture this way and that. The parents waited. The woman cleared her throat. The man shuffled his feet. The clock on the wall went tick-tick, tick-tick.

"I'll give you eight hundred and thirty *dordocs,*" the Madame said.

"Well...."

Miss Bestris bent forward, holding out the picture. "Here, then. Take it. I wouldn't offer that, but I need a girl right now. One of mine ran away last week, and I'm afraid she won't be able to work for a month or so after they bring her back. I'm being generous. Eight hundred and thirty, or take your picture and don't waste my time."

The man and woman stared at her. And the clock went *tick-tick.*

"Take it, Chav."

"All right," the man said. "We need the money."

Miss Bestris leaned across the desk, pressed a button on her panel. Almost immediately, a door slid silently open and her lawyer entered with a white, printed, standard-form sales contract in his hand. Efficiently and rapidly, he entered the particulars. "Sign here," he said, and the parents signed.

"Now," said the Madame, "if you'll bring in Lavada tomorrow at nine, I'll arrange for a doctor to be here. If his examination is satisfactory, the money will be ready."

The lawyer left, and the woman said, "You understand, we wouldn't do this but for—"

"I understand, perfectly," Miss Bestris said. "You don't need to worry. This is the best kind of house—Earthmen only, you know, and they're very particular. My girls are given the best of care. I'm like a mother to them, and if they are thrifty and diligent, they'll be able to save enough money in a—a very short time to redeem their contract as provided by law. You needn't worry at all."

"Well," the woman said, "I feel better after talking to you. I feel better about the whole thing to hear you talk like that."

The clock went *tick-tick.*

"Uh," the man said, "you won't—? That is, our little daughter is sometimes willful and ... uh ... well ... Sometimes."

Miss Bestris smiled. "We know how to handle girls."

"You'll treat her...?"

"As I would my own child," Miss Bestris said; she took out another cigarette, lit it. "I think we'll call her—well—Poppy. Earthmen like to feel at home, you know."

The clock went *tick-tick.*

"Well, uh," the man said. "Uh. Thank you."

★ ★ ★

In one of the rooms upstairs Mary sat before the dressing table with her back to the mirror, while June and Adele occupied the two overstuffed chairs. Night sounds drifted up from the yellow canal, and fresh flower scents whispered on the warm air. The diaphanous glass curtains rustled at the open window.

"They're too expensive," Mary said. "I'm sure Miss Bestris overcharges us for them."

"Hush," said June, glancing around at the walls nervously. "Hush, Mary." She smoothed at the delicate, plutolac lace fringe above her breasts. "Imported material like this costs money. You can't get it for nothing, and we have to have the best."

"I still think she charges too much."

Adele shrugged delicately and crossed shapely ankles. "I think Miss Bestris must like you, or she wouldn't let you wear that dress again tonight. You ought to watch out that you don't get on the wrong side of her."

Mary laughed, her amethyst eyes sparkling. "I won't care. Not after tonight."

"You're not going to run away?" June asked breathlessly. "You wouldn't dare do that. You'd catch it, sure!"

Mary shook her head. "Not *run* away."

Adele leaned forward and said huskily, "You got enough money to redeem your contract?"

Again Mary shook her head. "No. It's nine hundred and ten *dordocs.* I have only ninety-three. But I'll have enough in the morning!" She stood up and crossed to the window, looked out toward the spaceport.

"How?"

"Tell us, Mary!"

"Tell you what?" Anne asked, coming into the room. Languidly she drew the door closed behind her and rested against it. "Tell you what?" she insisted, narrowing milky eyes.

"Mary says she can redeem her contract tomorrow."

Anne's wide mouth curled contemptuously. "Nonsense!"

"It's not," said Mary without turning.

Anne glided sensuously across the room to the bed, her tight fitting plastic rippling with her tigerish muscles. She sat down.

"He said he'd take me away, this trip," Mary continued. "He'll sign off, and then we'll both get a ship and go to one of the frontier planets. Where it won't matter about—all this."

Anne laughed harshly. "My God! You believe *that?*"

"We've both been saving our money," Mary said dreamily. "He's in love with me. He said so."

"Honey, that's what they all say."

Smiling, Mary turned from the window and leaned backward, stretching. "You don't know him. He's different."

"They're all the same," Anne said, her mouth twisting bitterly. "They're just alike. Don't believe any of them."

And Mary said, "With him, it's different. You'll see."

After a moment, Anne said, "That Earthman? That what's-his-name?" Mary nodded, and Anne brushed an imaginary something off her knee. "An Earthman," Anne said. "They're the worst of all."

"You don't know him, or you wouldn't say that."

Adele looked away from Anne. "You love him, don't you, Mary?"

"Yes."

"You're a fool," Anne said. "Listen to me. *Love* a man? God! You'll see. After him, there'll be another and another, and—just like Rosy—you'll watch 'em leave you and laugh at you until finally you're hurt so bad you don't think you can stand being hurt any more, and then along comes another one, and it starts all over again, and then one night you take a razor blade and go to the sink and stick out your throat and...."

"No! No! You're wrong! He's not like the rest!"

Anne leaned back carelessly, resting, propped on one hand. "See. You know I'm right, already."

"You're not!"

Anne shrugged. "Honey, tell me that tomorrow night."

"I better go take my cake out," Mary said. She fled the room in a swirl of shimmering glastic.

Anne sneered, "I don't see why Miss Bestris puts up with her the way she does."

"You're jealous," June said quietly.

Anne did not answer.

"Mary's decent," Adele said. "Maybe that's why. She's from the sticks, and her parents still come to see her on visiting days, and there's something about her so— so innocent. Maybe that's why Miss Bestris likes her."

June said, "I think she's better than the rest of us. I think Miss Bestris feels sorry for her in a way."

"Don't make me laugh," Anne said, facing June. "The only one that'll ever feel sorry for her is herself!"

"You shouldn't have talked like that to her!" June snapped. "Why don't you let her alone? She'll feel bad enough without you helping!"

Anne rolled over on the bed and stared up at the ceiling. June took a helox lamp from her drawer and started to bake her hair darker. Those Earthmen were so funny about colors.

In the kitchen, Mary took the cake out of the oven. It was steamy and light and fluffy, and it smelled sweet and warm. She set it on the table and mixed a two-minute green frosting which she spread, carefully, over the cake. She patted here and there with the spatula and stood back, her eyes proud and serious.

She hummed a little tune under her breath as she scrubbed the pots and pans. Her hands moved in practiced rhythm, and the water splashed and gurgled. When the kitchen was again spotless, she looked once more at the cake, and then, turning out the light, she went back to her room.

Anne and Adele had left, but June was sitting quietly in the dusky moonlight. Her white dress seemed vaguely luminous.

Laughing, Mary flicked on the light.

"It's a wonderful cake," she said. "The best one I ever made. Just the way it should be."

"I wouldn't feel too bad, Mary, if he doesn't come to eat it," June said. "I don't want to sound like Anne, but there was a lot of sense in what she said."

"It's just like a real wedding cake." She hummed the snatch of Martian tune. "Like in the tele-papers." She laughed with her eyes. "The bridegroom takes the silver knife and cuts two large pieces of the cake while the bride, dressed in filament coral, stands at his right hand. She carries a bouquet of—Anne just likes to be mean!"

June frowned. Mary crossed to the dressing table. She studied her face in the mirror. It was heart shaped, elfin; her purple hair was a riot of curls, and her eyes were amethyst and gold. She smiled at herself. "I want to look as pretty as I can tonight." She twisted around. "You don't think he'll come either, do you?"

"I—no, Mary."

Mary looked back at the mirror. "He likes our canal blossom perfume." She dabbed some of it on her ear lobes. "I like it best, too."

June stood up, crossed to the musikon, found a slow five-toned waltz. She turned the music very low, and left the color mixer dim enough so that only the faintest ghosts projected hues moved on walls and ceiling.

Mary continued to stare into the mirror. "But he will come. I know it."

June said nothing.

"Don't you see? I just *know* he'll come."

June crossed back to her seat.

Mary turned from the mirror. "I'm sure he will. He's…."

June smiled wanly.

"Well, he will! You'll see!"

June said, "Even if it is an old dress, you look very nice in it."

"I've been learning his language. I can say 'thank you' and 'yes' and 'no' and 'I love you' and all kinds of things in it. He gave me a book, and I've been studying. I want to be able really to talk with him. We've got a lot to talk about. I want to find out about his parents, and what he likes for supper and what kind of music he likes to hear, and—and all sorts of things. I want to find out all about his planet, and—"

"Yes," June said wearily, "I know."

The music played on. The moving lights on the walls were like colored reflections from a sunlit river.

"He may be a little late tonight; he has a lot to do, first. But he'll be here."

Buzzzzz.

It was the red button; it blinked on and off.

"Visitors," June said.

"Look—" Mary said. "Look, June. I'm not half ready yet. Look. Tell Miss Bestris I'll be down a little late. Tell her I have a special boy, and it'll be all right. He wants me to wait for him."

June was on her feet. "All right. You'd better not wait too long!"

"I won't."

After June was gone, Mary returned to the task of making her face pretty, but after a moment, she turned from the mirror, leaned back, and tried to relax. Underneath her dress, her heart was pounding.

The warm air carried sounds of the night creatures. One of the great canal insects, screeching, flapped by the window. The tiny second moon crept up over the horizon, and the buildings cast double shadows.

Buzzz. Buzzzz.

Still Mary waited.

Buzzz. Buzzzz. Buzzzzzz.

She was afraid to wait any longer. But by now she was sure that he would be down stairs.

There was a last-minute flurry of combing and primping, and then she rustled out of the room, her head erect, her eyes shining.

★ ★ ★

The large reception room was filling. Overhead, the color organ threw shimmering, prismatic beams on the ceiling. Beneath it, stiff, embarrassed spacemen, mostly officers dressed in parade uniforms, chatted in space-pidgin with the laughing, rainbow-haired girls.

Miss Bestris sat in one corner, her eyes roving the room: settling here for a second, there for a second, checking, approving, disapproving, silently. Occasionally she would smile or nod at one of the girls or one of the spacemen, and once she frowned ever so slightly and shook her head.

Anne was reclining on a couch, eating a golden Martian apple, listening to a second mate; she played with a lock of his hair and smiled her wide smile.

June, angelic, sat primly in a straight-backed chair, the lieutenant at her feet, a boyish, space-pale Earthman, drew embarrassed circles on the carpet with his index finger.

In the next room, three couples were dancing to the slow music of an Earth orchestra.

An inner door opened, and a uniformed native sheriff stepped in, a crisp, military figure. "Miss Bestris?"

She stood up. "Yes?"

The Earthmen fell silent, waiting.

"We think we have your runaway." He turned to the door. "Bring her in."

Two more sheriffs entered, and between them, there was a young, slender girl. Her face was gaunt and tear-stained. Her body trembled. She looked at the Madame fearfully.

"You idiots!" Miss Bestris screamed. "Get her out of here! You'll ruin my party! Take her out!"

The two men removed the girl. To the remaining sheriff, Miss Bestris said, "Damn you, if you ever do anything like that again, I'll … I'll…."

"I'm sorry, Madame. But we wanted immediate identification. Would you want us to hold the wrong girl?"

"That's her, all right! Now, get out! Wait for me in my office."

When they were gone Miss Bestris turned to the silent room. In quite passable Esperanto she said, "I am sorry. A misunderstanding. I assure you, nothing. Go on with the party, and I'll see what I can do for the poor girl."

She stood up and in her own language said, "Lively, girls! Smile! You, Rita, hurry and serve tea!"

She made her exit.

The spacemen grumbled among themselves, coughed uneasily, watched the closed door through which the Madame had gone. Listening, they could hear only a muted mumble of sing-song sounds in several voices.

With determined animation, the girls moved about, smiled, chatted.

Rita came in, wheeling the tea tray, and the girls converged on it, each trying to be the first to serve her escort. The tea was the Martian stuff, concocted of a kind of local hemp. The Earthmen found it harsh and bitter to the taste, but gentle on the soul.

Anne had filled two cups and returned to the second mate when she caught sight of Mary coming down the stairs.

On the lowest step, Mary stood for a long time; her eyes eagerly searched the crowd. Slowly a puzzled, hurt look came over her face.

June came to her side after a little while.

"Isn't he here?"

"No. Not yet."

"I'm sorry," June said, touching Mary's arm lightly.

"It's all right. It's early yet. I'll just sit down by Miss Bestris' chair and wait for him."

She turned from June and went to the chair. Before she could sit down, a space corporal came over, bowed, and tried to take her hand. She shook her head. He smiled twistedly and walked stiffly away.

Another man smiled at her. She shook her head slowly.

Someone came in the front door, and she leaned forward. Then she slumped back limply.

She heard a tinkly laugh. She looked in its direction. She met Anne's eyes, bright and amused. Just then Miss Bestris came in, her eyes angry and her cheeks flushed. She strode across the room.

"Well," she said. "I'm glad to see you finally came down." She sank heavily into her chair. "Crescent's back. They just brought her in. The idiots came right in here with her. I'll bet I lost half-a-dozen customers. These Earthmen are sensitive about such things."

Mary was still staring at the door; Miss Bestris looked down at her.

"Well, what are you sitting here for?"

"Please, Miss Bestris. I'm waiting for my special boyfriend tonight."

She snorted and looked away. "Why isn't he here?"

"He will be."

"He'd better. I'll let you wait another—half an hour. That's all."

"Thank you, Miss Bestris. You're very kind to me."

"I indulge you more than I ought to, child," she said. "More than is good for you, if the truth were known."

A man came in; Mary stiffened and then relaxed.

The mutter of voices blended into a steady hum. More couples were dancing. Miss Bestris moved around the room. The music was tinny.

Another man came in.

"Your time's up," the Madame told Mary.

"Please, let me just wait for another few minutes."

Miss Bestris fixed her lips grimly. "I've had enough nonsense for tonight. You heard me!"

"*Please!*"

"You heard what I said."

"Miss Bestris, I couldn't. Not tonight. Honest, I couldn't. If I had to talk to anybody, I'd break down and cry. He'll come. I know he will."

Miss Bestris whirled on her. "Listen, you little—" But she stopped, suddenly. "All right," she said, gritting her teeth. "I can't afford another scene tonight. But you'll be sorry for this."

Miss Bestris stormily looked away. The dancers danced; the music swelled louder. Gradually, deliberately, the lights were waning.

"Haven't I always been good to you, Mary?" the Madame asked.

"Yes."

"Then like an obedient girl, do as I say. If he hasn't come by now, he just won't. He's gone to some other house."

"No!" Mary said doggedly.

"Just remember, tomorrow, how you deliberately disobeyed me. Your silly emotions are costing me money, and that's one thing I simply won't stand for."

"He'll come." Mary said. "You won't lose money."

Couples sat side by side, laughing, talking in whispers. Occasionally there were giggles. The room began to empty slowly.

The lights continued to dim until the rooms were gloomy. Even the shifting shades of the color organ were no more than a faint ambiance. Anne, laughing, helped her second mate to his feet.

"I'll give you one more chance," Miss Bestris said. "The next man that comes in…."

"No! I just couldn't! Not tonight!"

A few more customers drifted in. Then even the stragglers stopped coming. It was very late.

"He's deserted you; you see that now?" Madame Bestris sneered.

Mary stood up. There were tears in her eyes. "You can't—you don't— you don't know how I feel," she choked. "You don't care!" She turned and ran up the stairs, crying.

Several Earthmen, still in the big room, turned to watch. The torches were misty twinkles now. The last couples climbed the stairs and then Miss Bestris, too, went to bed.

★ ★ ★

The blue morning came. The town awoke; commerce began.

At seven, Miss Bestris lay in bed frowning, considering the events of the previous evening. But she was not so annoyed that she forgot to call a doctor on the teleview and arrange for him to come at nine to give a physical examination.

Her bulk out of bed, she dressed and went to the kitchen to brew a pot of hemp tea. The cleaning maid, moving about in the next room, heard Miss Bestris call sharply: "Flavia! Come in here!"

Flavia appeared with a dust rag in her hand.

"Did you cut this cake?"

"No, ma'am."

Miss Bestris glowered. "That little idiot! She must have slipped down here after we were all asleep and sat here and cried her silly little eyes out! If she thinks she can pull that love-sick act on me she'll soon find out different. Am I supposed to put up with having her moon over every space tramp that comes in? Why, I've taken more from her—!"

"Yes, ma'am."

Miss Bestris waddled to the stairs, climbed them determinedly. At Mary's door she stopped and twisted the knob. Locked!

Miss Bestris hammered. "Open up, Mary!" The door rattled under her hand. "Open that door at once!"

No answer.

Miss Bestris pounded harder. "Open up, I say!"

Anne sauntered into the hall, her dressing gown swishing. "She really made you look the fool last night, didn't she?" Anne said lazily.

"Mind your own business, slut!"

Anne smiled and shrugged.

"Open the door, Mary! Do you hear me! Open it!"

"Maybe she killed herself," Anne said. "It has happened."

"My God! No! She wouldn't dare. You think she would?"

Anne shrugged again. "They do funny things sometimes."

Miss Bestris' face was red. "Run down and get my keys. In my desk. You know where they are."

Then, "*For God's sake, hurry!*"

While she waited Miss Bestris rattled the door, pleading and cursing.

Finally Anne returned. Miss Bestris snatched the key with a shaking hand. She hurled the door open and burst inside.

"See here, you little—!" She stopped.

The room was empty.

On the neatly made bed reposed a little stack of money. When Miss Bestris got around to counting it, she found that it contained exactly nine hundred and ten *dordocs.*

Star Performer

by Robert J. Shea

Gavir gingerly fitted the round opening in the bottom of the silvery globe over the top of his hairless blue skull. He pulled the globe down until he felt tiny filaments touching his scalp. The tips of the wires were cold.

The moderator then said, "*Dreaming Through the Universe* tonight brings you the first native Martian to appear on the dreamwaves—Gavir of the Desert Men. With him is his guardian, Dr. Malcomb Rice, the noted anthropologist."

Then the moderator questioned Malcomb, while Gavir nervously awaited the moment when his thoughts would be transmitted to millions of Earthmen. Malcomb told how he had been struck by Gavir's intelligence and missionary-taught ability to speak Earth's language, and had decided to bring Gavir to Earth.

The moderator turned to Gavir. "Are you anxious to get back to Mars?"

No! Gavir thought. Back behind the Preserve Barrier that killed you instantly if you stepped too close to it? Back to the constant fear of being seized by MDC guards for a labor pool, to wind up in the MDC mines?

Mars was where Gavir's father had been pinned, bayonets through his hands and feet, to the wall of a shack just the other side of the Barrier, to die slowly, out of Gavir's reach. Father James told Gavir that the head of MDC himself had ordered the killing, because Gavir's father had tried to organize resistance to the Corporation. Mars was where the magic powers of the Earthmen and the helplessness of the Martian tribes would always protect the head of MDC from Gavir's vengeance.

Back to that world of hopeless fear and hatred? *I never want to go back to Mars! I want to stay here!*

But that wasn't what he was supposed to think. Quickly he said, "I will be happy to return to my people."

A movement caught his eye. The producer, reclining on a divan in a far corner of the small studio, was making some kind of signal by beating his fist against his forehead.

"Well, enough of that!" the moderator said briskly. "How about singing one of your tribal songs for us?"

Gavir said, "I will sing the *Song of Going to Hunt*." He heaved himself up from the divan, and, feet planted wide apart, threw back his head and began to howl.

He was considered a poor singer in his tribe, and he was not surprised that Malcomb and the moderator winced. But Malcomb had told him that it wouldn't matter. The dreamees receiving the dreamcast would hear the song as it *should* sound, as Gavir heard it in his mind. Everything that Gavir saw and heard and felt in his mind, the dreamees could see and hear and feel.

It was cold, bitter cold, on the plain. The hunter stood at the edge of the camp as the shriveled Martian sun struck the tops of the Shakam hills. The hunter hefted the long, balanced narvoon, the throwing knife, in his hand. He had faith in the knife, and in his skill with it.

The hunter filled his lungs, the cold air reaching deep into his chest. He shouted out his throat-bursting hunting cry. He began to run across the plain.

Crouching behind crumbling red rocks, racing over flat expanses of orange sand, the hunter sought traces of the seegee, the great slow desert beast whose body provided his tribe with all the essentials of existence. At last he saw tracks. He mounted a dune. Out on the plain before him a great brown seegee lumbered patiently, unaware of its danger.

The hunter was about to strike out after it, when a dark form leaped at him.

The hunter saw it out of the corner of his eye at the last moment. His startled sidestep saved him from the neck-breaking snap of the great jaws.

The drock's long body was armored with black scales. Curving fangs protruded from its upper jaw. Its hand-like forepaws ended in hooked claws, to grasp and tear its prey. It was larger, stronger, faster than the hunter. The thin Martian air carried weirdly high-pitched cries which proclaimed its craving to sink its fangs into the hunter's body. The drock's huge hind legs coiled back on their triple joints, and it sprang.

The hunter thrust the gleaming knife out before him, so that the dark body would land on its gleaming blade. The drock twisted in mid-air and landed to one side of the hunter.

Now, before it could gather itself for another spring, there was time for one cast of the blade. It had to be done at once. It had to be perfect. If it failed, the knife would be lost and the drock would have its kill. The hunter grasped the weapon by the blade, drew his arm back, and snapped it forward.

The blade struck deep into the throat of the drock.

The drock screamed eerily and jumped clumsily. The hunter threw himself at the great, dark body and retrieved the knife. He struck with it again and again into the gray twitching belly. Colorless blood ran out over the hard, tightly-stretched skin.

The drock fell, gave a last convulsion, and lay still. The hunter plunged the blade into the red sand to clean it. He threw back his head and bellowed his hunting cry. There was great glory in killing the drock, for it showed that the Desert Man and not the drock, was lord of the red waste.

Gavir sat down on the divan, exhausted, his song finished. He didn't hear the moderator winding up the dreamcast. Then the producer of the program was upon him.

He began shouting even before Gavir removed his headset. "What kind of a fool are you? Before you started that song, you dreamed things about the Martian Development Corporation that were libelous! I got the whole thing—the Barrier, the guards, the labor pools and mines, the father crucified. It was awful! MDC is one of our biggest sponsors."

Malcomb said, "You can't expect an untrained young Martian to control his very thoughts. And may I point out that your tone is hostile?"

At this a sudden change came over the producer. The standard Earth expression—invincible benignity—took control of his face. "I apologize for having spoken sharply, but dreamcasting is a nerve-wracking business. If it weren't for Ethical Conditioning, I don't know how I'd control my aggressive impulses. The Suppression of Aggression is the Foundation of Civilization, eh?"

Malcomb smiled. "Ethical Conditioning Keeps Society from Fissioning." He shook hands with the producer.

"Come around tomorrow at 1300 and collect your fee," said the producer. "Good night, gentlemen."

As they left the Global Dreamcasting System building, Gavir said to Malcomb, "Can we go to a bookstore tonight?"

"Tomorrow. I'm taking you to your hotel and then I'm going back to my apartment. We both need sleep. And don't forget, you've been warned not to go prowling around the city by yourself.

As soon as Gavir was sure that Malcomb was out of the hotel and well on his way home, he left his room and went out into the city.

In a pitifully few days he would be back in the Preserve, back with the fear of MDC, with hunger and the hopeless desire to find and kill the man who had ordered his father's death.

Now he had an opportunity to learn more about the universe of the Earthmen. Despite Malcomb's orders, he was going to find a seller of books.

During a reading class at the mission school, Father James had said, "In books there is power. All that you call magic in our Earth civilization is explained in books." Gavir wanted to learn. It was his only hope to find an alternative to the short, fear-ridden, impoverished life he foresaw for himself.

A river of force carried him, along with thousands of Earthmen—godlike beings in their perfect health and their impregnable benignity—through the streets of the city. Platforms of force raised and lowered him through the city's multiple levels.

And, as has always happened to outlanders in cities, he became lost.

★ ★ ★

He was in a quarter where furtive red and violet lights danced in the shadows of hunched buildings. A half-dozen Earthmen approached him, stopped and stared. Gavir stared back.

The Earthmen wore black garments and furs and metal ornaments. The biggest of them wore a black suit, a long black cape, and a broad-brimmed black hat. He carried a coiled whip in one hand. The Earthmen turned to one another.

"A Martian."

"Let's give pain and death to the Martian! It will be a new experience—one to savor."

"Take pain, Martian!"

The Earthman with the black hat raised his arm, and the long heavy lash fell on Gavir. He felt a savage sting in the arm he had thrown up to protect his eyes.

Gavir leaped at the Earthmen. He clubbed the man with the whip across the face. As the others rushed in, Gavir flailed about him with long arms and heavy fists.

He began to enjoy it. It was rare that a Martian had an opportunity to knock Earthmen down. The mood of the *Song of Going to Hunt* came over him. He sprang free of his attackers and drew his glittering narvoon.

The man with the whip yelled. They looked at his knife, and then all at once turned and ran. Gavir drew back his arm and threw the knife with a practiced catapult-snap of shoulder, elbow, and wrist. To his surprise, the blade clattered to the street far short of his retreating enemies. Then he remembered: you couldn't throw far in the gravity of Earth.

The Earthmen disappeared into a lift-force field. Gavir decided not to pursue them. He walked forward and picked up his narvoon, and saw that the street on which it lay was solid black pavement, not a force-field. He must be in the lowest level of the city. He didn't know his way around; he might meet more enemies. He forgot about the books he'd wanted, and began to search for his hotel.

★ ★ ★

When he got back to his room, he went immediately to bed. He slept late.

Malcomb woke him at 1100. Gavir told Malcomb about the strangely-dressed men who had tried to kill him.hat rat

"I told you not to wander around alone."

"But you did not tell me that Earthmen might try to kill me. You have told me that Earthmen are good and peace-loving, that there have been no acts of violence on Earth for many decades. You have told me that only the MDC men are exceptions, because they are living off Earth, and this somehow makes them different."

"Well, those people you ran into are another exception."

"Why?"

"You know about the Regeneration and Rejuvenation treatment we have here on Earth. A variation of it was given you to acclimate you to Earth's gravity and atmosphere. Well, since the R&R treatment was developed, we Earthmen have a life-expectancy of about one hundred fifty years. Those people who attacked you were Century-Plus. They are over a hundred years old, but as healthy, physically, as ever."

"What is wrong with them?"

"They seem to have outgrown their Ethical Conditioning. They live wildly. Violently. It's a problem without precedent, and we don't know what to do with them. The fact is, Senile Delinquency is our number one problem."

"Why not punish them?" said Gavir.

"They're too powerful. They are often people who've pursued successful careers and acquired a good deal of property and position. And there are getting to be more of them all the time. But come on. You and I have to go over to Global Dreamcasting and collect our fee."

★ ★ ★

The impeccably affable producer of *Dreaming Through the Universe* gave Malcomb a check and then asked them to follow him.

"Mr. Davery wants to see you. Mr. *Hoppy* Davery, executive vice-president in charge of production. Scion of one of Earth's oldest communications media families!"

They went with the producer to the upper reaches of the Global Dreamcasting building. There they were ushered into a huge office.

They found Mr. Hoppy Davery lounging on a divan the size of a space-port. He was youthful in appearance, as were all Earthmen, but a soft plumpness and a receding hairline made him look slightly older than average.

He pointed a rigid finger at Malcomb and Gavir. "I want you two to hear a condensed recording of statements taken from calls we received last night."

Gavir stiffened. They *had* gotten into trouble because of his thoughts about MDC.

A voice boomed out of the ceiling.

"That Martian boy has power. That song was a fist in the jaw. More!"

A woman's voice followed:

"If you let that boy go back to Mars I'll never dream a Global program again."

More voices:

"Enormous!"

"Potent!"

"That hunting song drove me mad. I *like* being mad!"

"Keep him on Earth."

Hoppy Davery pressed a button in the control panel on his divan, and the voices fell silent.

"Those callers that admitted their age were all Century-Plus. The boy appeals to the Century-Plus mentality. I want to try him again. This time on a really big dream-show, not just an educational 'cast. Got a spot on next week's Farfel Flisket Show. If he gets the right response, we talk about a contract. Okay?"

Malcomb said, "His visa expires—"

"We'll take care of his visa."

Gavir trembled with joy. Hoppy Davery pressed another button and a secretary entered with papers. She was followed by another woman.

The second woman was dark-haired and slender. She wore leather boots and tight brown breeches. She was bare from the waist up and her breasts were young and full. A jeweled clip fastened a scarlet cape at her neck. Her lips were a disconcertingly vivid red, apparently an artificial color. She kissed Hoppy Davery on the forehead, leaving red blotches on his pink dome. He wiped his forehead and looked at his hand.

"Do you have to wear that barbaric face-paint?" Hoppy turned sad eyes on Gavir and Malcomb. "Gentlemen, my mother, Sylvie Davery."

A Senile Delinquent! thought Gavir. She looked like Davery's younger sister. Malcomb stared at her apprehensively, and Gavir wondered if she were somehow going to attack them.

She looked at Gavir. "Mmm. What a body, what gorgeous blue skin. How tall are you, Blue Boy?"

"He's approximately seven feet tall, Sylvie," said Hoppy, "and what do you want here, anyway?"

"Just came up to see Blue Boy. One of the crowd dreamed him last night. Positively manic about him. I found out he'd be with you."

"See?" said Hoppy to Gavir. "The Century-Plus mentality. You've got something they go for. Undoubtedly because you're—forgive me—such a complete barbarian. That's what they're all trying to be."

"Spare me another lecture on Senile Delinquency, Our Number One Problem." She walked to the door and Gavir watched her all the way. She turned with a swirl of scarlet and a dramatic display of healthy young flesh. "See you again, Blue Boy."

After Sylvie left, Hoppy Davery said, "That might be a good professional name—Blue Boy. Gavir doesn't *mean* anything. Now what kind of a song could you do for the Farfel Flisket show?"

Gavir thought. "Perhaps you would like the *Song of Creation.*"

"It's part of a fertility rite," Malcomb explained.

"Great! Give the Senile Delinquents another workout. It's not quite ethical, but it's good for us. But for heaven's sake, Blue Boy, keep your mind off MDC!"

★ ★ ★

The following week, Gavir sang the *Song of Creation* on the Farfel Flisket show, and transmitted the images which it brought up in his mind to his audience. A jubilant Hoppy Davery called him at his hotel next morning.

"Best response I've ever seen! The Century-Plussers have been rioting and throwing mass orgies ever since you sang. But they take time out to call us up and beg for more. I've got a sponsor and a two-year contract lined up for you."

The sponsor was pacing back and forth in Hoppy Davery's office when Malcomb and Gavir arrived. Hoppy introduced him proudly. "Mr. Jarvis Spurling, president of the Martian Development Corporation."

Gavir's hand leaped at the narvoon under his doublet.

Then he stopped himself. He turned the gesture into the proffer of a handshake. "How do you do?" he said quietly. In his mind he congratulated himself. He had learned emotional control from the Earthmen. Here was the man who had ordered his father crucified! Yet he had managed to hide his instant desire to strike, to kill, to carry out the oath of the blood feud then and there.

Jarvis Spurling ignored Gavir's hand and stared coldly at him. There was not a trace of the usual Earthman's kindliness in his square, battered face. "I'm told you got talent. Okay, but a Bluie is a Bluie. I'll pay you because a Bluie on Dreamvision is good publicity for MDC products. But one slip like on your first 'cast and you go back to the Preserve."

"Mr. Spurling!" said Malcomb. "Your tone is hostile!"

"Damn right. That Ethical Conditioning slop doesn't work on me. I've lived too long on the frontier. And I know Bluies."

I will sign the contract," said Gavir.

As he drew his signature pictograph on the contract, Sylvie Davery sauntered in. She held a white tube between her painted lips. The end of the tube was glowing and giving off clouds of smoke. Hoppy Davery coughed and Sylvie winked at Gavir. Gavir straightened up, and she took a long look at his seven feet.

"All finished, Blue Boy? Come on, let's go have a drink at Lucifer Grotto."

Caution told Gavir to refuse. But before he could speak Spurling snapped, "Disgusting! An Earth woman and a Bluie! If you were on Mars, lady, we'd deport you so fast your tail would burn. And God help the Bluie!"

Sylvie blew a cloud of smoke at Spurling. "You're not on Mars, Jack. You're back in civilization where we do what we damned well please."

Spurling laughed. "I've heard about you Century-Plussers. You're all sick."

"You can't claim any monopoly on mental health. Not with that concentration camp you run on Mars. Coming, Gavir?"

Gavir grinned at Spurling. "The contract, I believe, does not cover my private life."

Hoppy Davery said, "Sylvie, I don't think this is wise."

Sylvie uttered a short, sharp obscenity, linked arms with Gavir, and strolled out.

"You screwball Senile Delinquent," Spurling yelled after Sylvie, "you oughtta be locked up!"

★ ★ ★

Lucifer Grotto was in that same quarter in which Gavir had been attacked. Sylvie told him it was *the* hangout for wealthier New York Century-Plussers. Gavir told her about the attack, and she laughed. "It won't happen again. You're a hero to the Senile Delinquents now. By the way, the big fellow with the broad-brimmed hat, he's one of the most prominent Senile Delinquents of our day. He's president of the biggest privately-owned space line, but he likes to call himself the Hat Rat. You must be one of the few people who ever got away from him alive."

"He seemed happy to get away from me," said Gavir.

An arrangement of force-planes and 3V projections made the front of Lucifer Grotto appear to be a curtain of flames. Gavir hung back, but Sylvie inserted a tiny gold pitchfork into a small aperture in the glowing, rippling surface. The flames swept aside, revealing a doorway. A bearded man in black tights escorted them through a luridly-lit bar to a private room. When they were alone, Sylvie dropped her cape to the floor, sat on the edge of a huge, pink divan, and smiled at Gavir.

Gavir contemplated her. That she was over a hundred years old was a little frightening. But the skin of her face and her bare upper body was a warm color, and tautly filled. She had lashed out at Spurling, and he liked her for that. But in one way she was like Spurling. She didn't fit into the bland, non-violent world of Malcomb and Hoppy.

He shook his head. He said, "Sylvie, why—well, why are you the way you are? Why—and how—have you broken away from Ethical Conditioning?"

Sylvie frowned. She spoke a few words into the air, ordering drinks. She said, "I didn't do it deliberately. When I reached the age of about a hundred it stopped working for me. I suddenly wanted to do what *I* wanted to do. And then I found out that I didn't *know* what I wanted to do. It was Ethical Conditioning or nothing, so I picked nothing. And here I am, chasing nothing."

"How do you chase nothing?"

She set fire to a white tube. "This, for instance. They used to do it before they found out it caused cancer. Now there's no more cancer, but even if there were, I'd still smoke. That's the attitude I have. You try things. You live in the past, if you're inclined, adopt the costumes and manners of some more colorful time. You try ridiculous things, disgusting things, vicious things. You know they're all nothing, but you have to do something, so you go on doing nothing, elaborately and violently."

A tray of drinks rose through the floor. Sylvie frowned as she noticed a folded paper tucked between the glasses. She picked it up and read it, chuckled, and read it again, aloud.

"Sir: I beg you to forgive the presumption of my recent attack on you. Since then you have captured my imagination. I now hold you to be the noblest savage of them all. Henceforward please consider me, your obedient servant, Hat Rat."

"You've impressed him," said Sylvie. "But you impress me even more. Come here."

She held out slim arms to him. He had no wish to refuse her. She was not like a Martian woman, but he found the differences exciting and attractive. He went to her, and he forgot entirely that she was over a hundred years old.

★ ★ ★

In the months that followed, Gavir's fame spread over Earth. By spring, the rating computers credited him with an audience of eight hundred million—ninety-five percent of whom were Century-Plussers. Davery doubled Gavir's salary.

Gavir toured the world with Sylvie, mobbed everywhere by worshipful Century-Plussers. Male Century-Plussers by the millions adopted blue doublets and blue kilts in honor of their hero.

Blue-dyed hair was now *de rigueur* among the ladies of Lucifer Grotto. The Hat Rat himself, who often appeared at a respectful distance in crowds around Gavir, now wore a wide-brimmed hat of brightest blue.

Then there came the dreamcast on which Gavir sang the *Song of Complaint.*

It was an ancient song, a Desert Man's outcry against injustice, enemies, false friends and callous leaders. It was a protest against sufferings that could neither be borne nor prevented. At the climax of the song Gavir pictured a tribal chief who refused to make fair division of the spoils of a hunt with his warriors. Gradually he allowed this image to turn into a picture of Hoppy Davery withholding bundles of money from a starving Gavir. Then he ended the song.

Hoppy sent for him next morning.

"Why did you do that?" he said. "Listen to this."

A recorded voice boomed: "This is Hat Rat. Pay the Blue Boy what he deserves, or I will give you death. It will be a personal thing between you and me. I will besprinkle you with corrosive acids; I will burn out your eyes; I will—"

Hoppy cut the voice off. Gavir saw that he was sweating. "There were *dozens* like that. If you want more money, I'll *give* you more money. Say something nice about me on your next dreamcast, for heaven's sake!"

Gavir spread his big blue hands. "I am sorry. I don't want more money. I cannot always control the pictures I make. These images come into my mind even though they have nothing to do with me."

Hoppy shook his head. "That's because you haven't had Ethical Conditioning. We don't have this trouble with our other performers. You just must remember that dreamvision is the most potent communications medium ever devised. Be *careful!*"

"I will," said Gavir.

★ ★ ★

In his next dreamcast Gavir sang the *Song of the Blood Feud.* He pictured a Desert Man whose father had been killed by a drock.

The Desert Man ran over the red sand, and he found the drock. He did not throw his knife. That would not have satisfied his hatred. He fell upon the drock and stabbed and stabbed.

The Desert Man howled his hunting-cry over the body of his enemy, and spat into its face.

And the fanged face of the drock turned into the square, battered face of Jarvis Spurling. Gavir held the image in his mind for a long moment.

When the dreamcast was over, a studio page ran up to Gavir. "Mr. Spurling wants to see you at once, at his office."

"Let him come and find me," said Gavir. "Let us go, Sylvie."

They went to Lucifer Grotto, where Gavir's wealthiest admirers among the Senile Delinquents were giving a party for him in the Pandemonium Room. The only prominent person missing, as Sylvie remarked after surveying the crowd, was the Hat Rat. They wondered about it, but no one knew where he was.

Sheets of flame illuminated the wild features and strange garments of over a hundred Century-Plus ladies and gentlemen. Gouts of flame leaped from the walls to light antique-style cigarettes. Drinks were refilled from nozzles of molded fire.

An hour passed from the time of Gavir's arrival.

Then Jarvis Spurling joined the party. There was a heavy frontier sonic pistol strapped at his waist. A protesting Malcomb was behind him.

Jarvis Spurling's square face was dark with anger. "You deliberately put my face on that animal! You want to make the public hate me. I pay your salary and keep you here on Earth, and this is what I get for it. All right. A Bluie is a Bluie, and I'll treat you like a Bluie should be treated." He unsnapped his holster and drew the square, heavy pistol out and pointed it at Gavir.

Gavir stood up. His right hand plucked at his doublet.

"You're itching to go for that throwing knife," said Spurling. "Go on! Take it out and get ready to throw it. I'll give you that much chance. Let's make a game out of this. We'll make like we're back on Mars, Bluie, and you're out hunting a drock. And you find one, only this drock has a gun. How about that, Bluie?"

Gavir took out the narvoon, grasped the blade, and drew his arm back.

"Gavir!"

It was the Hat Rat. He stood between pillars of flame in the doorway of the Pandemonium Room of Lucifer Grotto, and there was a peculiar contrivance of dark brown wood and black metal tubing cradled in his arm. "This ancient shotgun I dedicate to your blood feud. I shall hunt down your enemy, Gavir!"

Spurling turned. The Hat Rat saw him.

"The enemy!" the Hat Rat shouted.

The shotgun exploded.

Spurling's body was thrown back against Gavir. Gavir saw a huge ragged red caved-in place in Spurling's chest. Spurling's body sagged to the floor and lay there face up, eyes open. The Senile Delinquents of Lucifer Grotto leaned forward to grin at the tattered body.

Still holding the narvoon, Gavir stood over his dead enemy. He threw back his head and howled out the hunting cry of the Desert Men. Then he looked down and spat in Jarvis Spurling's dead face.

Blind Spot

by Bascom Jones, Jr.

Johnny Stark, director of the department of Interplanetary Relations for Mars' Settlement One, reread the final paragraph of the note which he had found on his desk, upon returning from lunch earlier in the day.

His eye flicked rapidly over the moistly smeared Martian scrawl, ignoring the bitterness directed at him in the first paragraphs. He was vaguely troubled by the last sentences. But he hadn't been able to pin the feeling down.

> *... Our civilization predates that of Earth's by millions of years. We are an advanced, peaceful race. Yet, since Earth's first rocket landed here thirteen years ago, we have been looked upon as freaks and contemptuously called 'bug-men' behind our backs! This is our planet. We gave of our far-advanced knowledge and science freely, so that Earth would be a better place. We asked nothing in return, but we were rewarded by having forced upon us foreign ideas of government, religion, and behavior. Our protests have been silenced by an armed-police and punitive system we've never before needed. Someday you will awaken to this injustice. On that day in your life, you have my sympathy and pity!*

Stark knew that the Settlement's Investigations Lab could readily determine the identity of the Martian who had written the note. But he hesitated to send it over. Under the New System, such troublemakers were banished to the slave-labor details of the precious-earth mines to the North.

Crumpling the note in sudden decision, Stark dropped it into the office incendiary tube. The morning visi-report had shown that there were more than 17,000 workers at the mines. Only five had been Earthlings. Let the armed-police system find the Martian through their own channels. It wasn't his job.

A glance at the solar clock on the far wall reminded him there was still time for one more interview before the last bell, so he impatiently signaled his secretary to send in the waiting couple.

Ordinarily, he liked his work and time meant little to him. He had jumped from interpreter to director in the ten years since the department had been created. But this day was different.

Stark was to announce his engagement at the Chief's monthly dinner party that evening and time had seemed to drag since his lunch with Carol.

When the door opened, he rose and nodded to the plump, freckle-faced girl who entered. The girl topped five feet by one or two inches, but she was no taller than the Martian man who followed her at the prescribed four feet.

After the girl had seated herself, Stark and the Martian sat down. Stark opened the folder, which his secretary had placed on his desk earlier.

"Your names are Ruth and Ralph Gilraut? And you want permission to move into Housing Perimeter D?" It was merely a formality, since the information was in the folder.

When the girl nodded, Stark placed a small check mark in the space beside her name. Then he turned to the Martian.

The large, single red eye set deep in the Martian's smooth, green forehead above the two brown ones blinked twice before he answered.

He spoke deliberately. "As is required of all Martians under the New System, I have taken the name of one of the early Earthlings to write and pronounce." The large red eye blinked again. "My wife would like to move into Housing Perimeter D. By regulation, I respect her wish."

Stark placed a check mark by the Martian's name. He wiped the smudge of ink off his hand and said, "You both know, of course, that Perimeter D is reserved for couples who have intermarried and are about to have offspring?"

The girl and the Martian nodded, and the girl passed Stark a medical report. Stark looked over the report and then made a notation on a small pink slip.

He said, "This permit certifies that you are eligible to move from Perimeter E to Housing Perimeter D. It also certifies that your husband has no record as a troublemaker." Stark looked at the girl. "You understand that you may visit your friends in Perimeter E, but, by law, they will not be allowed to enter Perimeter D to visit you. And, of course, the new law clearly states that neither of you may visit Earthlings in Housing Perimeter A, B or C."

The girl looked down at her hands. Her voice was almost inaudible. "My husband and I are familiar with the advantages and disadvantages listed under the section pertaining to intermarriage in the new law, Mr. Stark. Thank you."

Stark rose as they left. For a brief moment, he thought he had detected a sense of rebellion in their attitude. But that was not possible.

The new law provided equality for all. And his department had been created to iron out relations between the two races—excepting complaints originated by troublemakers for the purpose of weakening the New System. In such cases,

Investigations had stepped in and the Martian or Earthling troublemaker had been sent to the rare-earth mines.

The reddish light filtering in through the quartz and lead wall of his office showed that it was almost time for the last bell.

On the street below, shoppers were streaming out of the stores on their way to the various housing perimeters.

Earthlings were climbing into their speedy little jet cars for the short trip to the recently modernized inner perimeters. Martians were waiting for the slower auto buses. The traffic problem had been solved, under the New System, by restricting the use of the Martian-built jet cars to persons living in the inner perimeters.

As Stark watched, a black jet car impatiently hurtled out of the line of traffic, bowled through a crowd of Martians waiting for an auto bus, and skidded to a stop at the curb in front of the building.

A tall girl got out. The red evening glow reflecting from her golden hair, made her breathing globe almost amber. Male Martians and Earthlings alike turned to stare in appreciation as she pushed her way through the crowd to the building's compressor lock. Carol was that kind of girl.

★ ★ ★

Almost at the exact moment that Carol opened the door into Stark's office, the yellow visi-screen of the vocal box upon Stark's desk flashed on brilliantly and the Chief's booming voice filled the office. The light from the screen picked up the highlights on the furniture and gave a sallow, greenish cast to Stark's features. Carol stepped back into the doorway to stay out of range of the two-way unit.

"Stark!" The automatic tuner on the box corrected to bring the Chief's image in wire-sharp focus.

"Yes, sir?"

"About the dinner tonight. Just checking to make sure you're planning to be there. We want a full turnout. An inspection team has come up from Earth and we have two visiting dignitaries from Venus."

Stark nodded and waited for the Chief to say something else, but the visi-screen blanked out.

Carol said, "That was Dad, wasn't it?"

Stark felt very depressed suddenly. "Haven't you told him yet?"

"No. He's been tied up with those inspectors all afternoon. And you know how Dad is, Johnny. There's a right and a wrong time to tell him things. Right now, he's only interested in hearing about Earth."

"But we're supposed to announce our engagement tonight at the dinner." He shook his head. "We can't go on forever with just a few stolen moments here and there, eating an occasional lunch or third meal together in little out-of-the-way places."

Carol laughed, the youthful swell of her breasts against the soft, spun-glass material of her blouse. "Don't worry so, Johnny! I'm a big girl now. This is my eighteenth birthday. Dad's bark is much worse than his bite. I'll tell him about us on the way home."

She moved closer to him, until he could feel the warmth of her body. He could see the warm, damp indentation where her breathing globe had rested against her shoulders and chest.

She asked teasingly, "What did you get me for my birthday, Johnny? Something real nice?"

"What did you want?" Johnny asked her gently.

And suddenly she wasn't teasing any more. She put her arms around him. "Dad and my brother would say I'm crazy. But all I want, Johnny, is you. Just you! You know that."

Stark had picked out her birthday present, but he wanted it to be a surprise for that night. He said, "I already saw one of your presents. A black jet car!"

"How did you know that?"

"I saw you drive up in it a few minutes ago."

Carol giggled. "Dad gave it to me. Did you see me plow through that crowd waiting for the auto bus?"

"Did your brother send you anything?"

She nodded. "Three new outfits from Earth. They were on the same liner that brought the inspection team to the Settlement this morning. Oh, yes, and the captain of the liner brought me this."

She showed him the tiny pin she wore attached to her collar. The pin itself was a carefully wrought but cruel caricature of an awkward bug-like creature. A small ruby set in the center of its face served as its eye.

Stark frowned. "Carol, you shouldn't be wearing that." He reached up and unpinned it. "That's the sort of thing our department is fighting."

"But the captain said it was the latest rage back on Earth. They're even making toys like it. I'm sure they're not designed to poke fun at anyone."

Stark started to say something, but the last bell interrupted him. He said, "If you're going to take your father home and tell him about us before the dinner, you'd better hurry. I'll come early."

Carol kissed him and said good-by. She left the pin on Stark's desk and was smiling at him as she closed the door.

★ ★ ★

After waiting until the first rush of workers had gone and the building was quiet, Stark caught the elevator down. The overhead lights in the compressor lock were reflected in the twin rows of breathing globes. The green-tinted ones had to be used by Martians in the building, and the clear ones were used by Earthmen when they were outside in the Martian atmosphere. Stark stopped in at a little open shop down one of the many side streets. The sign said "Closed," but he rang the bell until a little, dried-up Martian appeared.

The storekeeper handed him a small box. Stark opened it to examine the ring—Carol's birthday present. The single, large diamond set in the thin precious-metal band dated back to an all-but-forgotten custom practiced on Earth. Stark thought the engagement ring would please Carol, though.

Standing in the compressor lock at the Chief's home later, Stark rubbed the diamond against the sleeve of his tunic. He fumbled with his breathing globe and then pushed the button that activated the door. The tele-guard beyond the opening door scanned him rapidly. As he stepped forward, a red light above the tele-guard flashed on and the door began to close again.

Stark threw all his strength against the door and squeezed through into the house.

Throughout the house, Stark could hear the alarm bell. A taped voice, activated by the tele-guard, said, "Do not enter! Do not enter!"

He found Carol and the Chief in the library alone. Nearly purple with rage, the Chief drew himself up to his full six feet.

The Chief bellowed, "Stark! Are you crazy?"

The growing feeling of sickness spread through Stark.

"Who do you think you are?" the Chief yelled. "Get back to your office and consider yourself under arrest as a troublemaker. Give you people an inch and you try to walk away with everything. Why, I wouldn't let you touch my daughter if you were the last living being in the Universe!"

Carol didn't look up. She stood through it all, silently, without moving. Stark knew now where his blind spot had been. He turned and left them.

Back at his office, he waited for the police. Stark stared down at his reflection in the polished top of the desk. A yellow, moist film of sweat covered his face. The red eye set in his forehead blinked. But the pain visible just behind the surface of that eye was not over Carol or himself.

The pain was for what he was seeing for the first time.

THE SETTLERS

One Martian Afternoon

by Tom Leahy

The clod burst in a cloud of red sand and the little Martian sand dog ducked quickly into his burrow. Marilou threw another at the aperture in the ground and then ran over and with the inside of her foot she scraped sand into it until it was filled to the surface. She started to leave, but stopped.

The little fellow might choke to death, she thought, it wasn't his fault she had to live on Mars. Satisfied that the future of something was dependent on her whim, she dug the sand from the hole. His little yellow eyes peered out at her.

"Go on an' live," she said magnanimously.

She got up and brushed the sand from her knees and dress, and walked slowly down the red road.

The noon sun was relentless; nowhere was there relief from it. Marilou squinted and shaded her eyes with her hand. She looked in the sky for one of those infrequent Martian rain clouds, but the sky was only occasionally spotted by fragile white puffs. Like the sun, they had no regard for her, either. They were too concerned with moving toward the distant mountains, there to cling momentarily to the peaks and then continue on their endless route.

Marilou dabbed the moisture from her forehead with the hem of her dress. "I know one thing," she mumbled. "When I grow up, I'll get to Earth an' never come back to Mars, no matter what!"

She broke into a defiant, cadenced step.

"An' I won't care whether you an' Mommy like it or not!" she declared aloud, sticking out her chin at an imaginary father before her.

Before she realized it, a tiny, lime-washed stone house appeared not a hundred yards ahead of her. That was the odd thing about the Martian midday; something small and miles away would suddenly become large and very near as you approached it.

The heat waves did it, her father had told her. "Really?" she had replied, then immediately thought, *You think you know so doggone much.*

★ ★ ★

"Aunt Twylee!" She broke into a run. By the Joshua trees, through the stone gateway she ran, and with a leap she lit like a young frog on the porch. "Hi, Aunt Twylee!" she said breathlessly.

An ancient Martian woman sat in a rocking chair in the shade of the porch. She held a bowl of purple river apples in her lap. Her papyrus-like hands moved quickly as she shaved the skin from one. In a matter of seconds it was peeled. She looked up over her bifocals at the panting Marilou.

"Gracious, child, you shouldn't run like that this time of day," she said. "You Earth children aren't used to our Martian heat. It'll make you sick if you run too much."

"I don't care! I hate Mars! Sometimes I wish I could just get good an' sick, so's I'd get to go home!"

"Marilou, you are *such* a little tyrant!" Aunt Twylee laughed.

"Watcha' doin', Aunt Twylee?" Marilou asked, getting up from her frog posture and coming near the old Martian lady's chair.

"Oh, peeling apples, dear. I'm going to make a cobbler this afternoon." She dropped the last apple, peeled, into the bowl. "There, done. Would you like a little cool apple juice, Marilou?"

"You betcha! Hey, could I watch you make the cobbler, Aunt Twylee, could I? Mommy can't make it for anything. It tastes like glue. Maybe, if I could see how you do it, maybe I could show her. Do you think?"

"Now, Marilou, your mother must be a wonderful cook to have raised such a healthy little girl. I'm sure there's nothing she could learn from me," Aunt Twylee said as she arose. "Let's go inside and have that apple juice."

The kitchen was dark and cool, and filled with the odors of the wonderful edibles the old Martian had created on and in the Earth-made stove. She opened the Earth-made refrigerator that stood in the corner and withdrew an Earth-made bottle filled with Martian apple juice.

Marilou jumped up on the table and sat cross-legged.

"Here, dear." Aunt Twylee handed her a glass of the icy liquid.

"Ummm, thanks," Marilou said, and gulped down half the contents. "That tastes dreamy, Aunt Twylee."

The little girl watched the old Martian as she lit the oven and gathered the necessary ingredients for the cobbler. As she bent over to get a bowl from the shelf beneath Marilou's perch, her hair brushed against the child's knee. Her hair was soft, soft and white as a puppy's, soft and white like the down from a dandelion. She smiled at Marilou. She always smiled; her pencil-thin mouth was a perpetual arc.

Marilou drained the glass. "Aunt Twylee, is it true what my daddy says about the Martians?"

"True? How can I say, dear? I don't know what he said."

"Well, I mean, that when us Earth people came, you Martians did inf… infan…"

"Infanticide?" Aunt Twylee interrupted, rolling the dough on the board a little flatter, a little faster.

"Yes, that's it. He said you killed babies." Marilou took an apple from the bowl. "My daddy says you were real primitive, an' killed your babies for some silly religious reason. I think that's awful! How could it be religious? God couldn't like to have little babies killed!" She took a big bite of the apple; the juice ran from the corners of her mouth.

"Your daddy is a very smart man, Marilou, but he's partially wrong. It is true, but not for religious reasons. It was a necessity. You must remember, dear, Mars is very arid—sterile—unable to sustain many living things. It *was* awful, but it was the only way we knew to control the population."

Marilou looked down her button nose as she picked a brown spot from the apple. "Hmmph, I'll tell 'im he's wrong," she said. "He thinks he knows so damn much!"

"Marilou!" Aunt Twylee exclaimed as she looked over her glasses. "A sweet child like you shouldn't use such language!"

Marilou giggled and popped the remaining portion of the apple in her mouth.

"Do your parents know where you are, child?" Aunt Twylee asked, as she took the bowl from Marilou's hands. She began dicing the apples into a dough-lined casserole.

"No, they don't," Marilou replied. She sprayed the air with little particles of apple as she talked. "Everybody's gone to the hills to look for the boys."

"The boys?" Aunt Twylee stopped her work and looked at the little girl.

"Yes. Jimmy an' Eddie an' some of the others disappeared from the settlement this morning. The men're afraid they've run off to th' hills an' the renegades got 'em."

"Gracious," Aunt Twylee said; her brow knitted into a criss-cross of wrinkles.

"Oh, I know those dopes. They're prob'ly down at th' canals fishin' or somep'n."

"Just the same, your mother will be frantic, dear. You should have told her where you were going."

"I don't care," Marilou said with unadulterated honesty. "She'll be all right when I get home."

Aunt Twylee shook her head and clucked her tongue.

"Can I have another glass? Please?"

The old lady poured the glass full again. And then she sprinkled sugar down among the apple cubes in the casserole and covered them with a blanket of dough. She cut an uneven circle of half-moons in it and put it in the oven. "There—all ready to bake, Marilou," she sighed.

"It looks real yummy, Aunt Twylee."

"Well, I certainly hope it turns out good, dear," she said, wiping her forehead with her apron. She looked out the open back door. The landscape was beginning to gray as heavier clouds moved down from the mountains and pressed the afternoon heat closer, more oppressively to the ground. "My, it's getting hot. I wouldn't be a bit surprised if we didn't get a little rain this afternoon, Marilou." She turned back to the little girl. "Tell me some more about your daddy, dear. We Martians certainly owe a lot to men like your father."

"That's what he says too. He says, you Martians would have died out in a few years, if we hadn't come here. We're so much more civi… civili…"

"Civilized?"

"Yeah. He says, we were so much more 'civ-ilized' than you that we saved your lives when we came here with all our modern stuff."

"Well, that's true enough, dear. Just look at that wonderful Earth stove," Aunt Twylee said, and laughed. "We wouldn't be able to bake an apple cobbler like that without it, would we?"

A rumble of thunder shouldered through the crowded, hot air.

"No. He says, you Martians are kinda likeable, but you can't be trusted. He's nuts! *I* like you Martians!"

"Thank you, child, but everyone's entitled to his own opinion. Don't judge your daddy too severely," Aunt Twylee said as she scraped spilled sugar from the table and put little bits of it on her tongue.

"He says that you'd bite th' hand that feeds you. He says, we brought all these keen things to Mars, an' that if you got th' chance, you'd kill all of us!"

"Gracious," said Aunt Twylee as she speared scraps of dough with the point of her long paring knife.

"He's a dope!" Marilou said.

Aunt Twylee opened the oven and peeked in at the cobbler. The aroma of the simmering apples rushed out and filled the room.

"Could I have some cobbler when it's done?" Marilou asked, her mouth filling with saliva.

"I'm afraid not, child. It's getting rather late."

The thunder rumbled again—a little closer, a little louder.

The old lady washed the blade of the knife in the sink. "Tell me more of what your father says, dear," she said as she adjusted the bifocals on her thin nose and ran her thumb along the length of the knife's blade.

"Oh, nothin' much more. He just says that you'd kill us if you had th' chance. That's the way the inferior races always act, he says. They want to kill th' people that help 'em, 'cause they resent 'em."

"Very interesting."

"Well, it isn't so, is it, Aunt Twylee?"

The room was filled with blinding blue-white light, and the walls quaked at the sound of a monstrous thunderclap.

The old Martian glanced nervously at the clock on the wall. "My, it *is* getting late," she said as she fondled the knife in her hands.

"You Martians wouldn't do anything like that, would you?"

"You want the truth, don't you, dear?" Aunt Twylee asked, smiling, as she walked to the table where Marilou sat.

"'Course I do, Aunt Twylee," she said.

Her scream was answered and smothered by the horrendous roar of the thunder, and the piercing hiss of the rain that fell in sheets. In great volumes of water, it fell, as though the heavens were attempting to wash the sins of man from the universe and into non-existence in the void beyond the void.

★ ★ ★

Marilou lay beside Jimmy, Eddie, and the other children. Aunt Twylee smiled at them, closed the bedroom door and returned to the kitchen.

The storm had moved on; the thunder was the faint grumbling of a pacified old man. What water fell was a monotonous trickle from the eaves of the lime-washed stone house. Aunt Twylee washed the blood from the knife and wiped it dry on her apron. She opened the oven and took out the browned cobbler. Sweet apple juice bubbled to the surface through the half-moons and burst in delights of sugary aroma. The sun broke through the thinning edge of the thunderhead.

Aunt Twylee brushed a lock of her feathery white hair from her moist cheek. "Gracious," she said, "I must tidy up a bit before the others come."

The Statue

by Mari Wolf

"Lewis," Martha said. "I want to go home."

She didn't look at me. I followed her gaze to Earth, rising in the east.

It came up over the desert horizon, a clear, bright star at this distance. Right now it was the Morning Star. It wasn't long before dawn.

I looked back at Martha sitting quietly beside me with her shawl drawn tightly about her knees. She had waited to see it also, of course. It had become almost a ritual with us these last few years, staying up night after night to watch the earthrise.

She didn't say anything more. Even the gentle squeak of her rocking chair had fallen silent. Only her hands moved. I could see them trembling where they lay folded in her lap, trembling with emotion and tiredness and old age. I knew what she was thinking. After seventy years there can be no secrets.

We sat on the glassed-in veranda of our Martian home looking up at the Morning Star. To us it wasn't a point of light. It was the continents and oceans of Earth, the mountains and meadows and laughing streams of our childhood. We saw Earth still, though we had lived on Mars for almost sixty-six years.

"Lewis," Martha whispered softly. "It's very bright tonight, isn't it?"

"Yes," I said.

"It seems so near."

She sighed and drew the shawl higher about her waist.

"Only three months by rocket ship," she said. "We could be back home in three months, Lewis, if we went out on this week's run."

I nodded. For years we'd watched the rocket ships streak upward through the thin Martian atmosphere, and we'd envied the men who so casually travelled from world to world. But it had been a useless envy, something of which we rarely spoke.

Inside our veranda the air was cool and slightly moist. Earth air, perfumed with the scent of Earth roses. Yet we knew it was only illusion. Outside, just beyond the glass, the cold night air of Mars lay thin and alien and smelling of alkali. It seemed to me tonight that I could smell that ever-dry Martian dust, even here. I sighed, fumbling for my pipe.

"Lewis," Martha said, very softly.

"What is it?" I cupped my hands over the match flame.

"Nothing. It's just that I wish—I wish we *could* go home, right away. Home to Earth. I want to see it again, before we die."

"We'll go back," I said. "Next year for sure. We'll have enough money then."

She sighed. "Next year may be too late."

I looked over at her, startled. She'd never talked like that before. I started to protest, but the words died away before I could even speak them. She was right. Next year might indeed be too late.

Her work-coarsened hands were thin, too thin, and they never stopped shaking any more. Her body was a frail shadow of what it had once been. Even her voice was frail now.

She was old. We were both old. There wouldn't be many more Martian summers for us, nor many years of missing Earth.

"Why can't we go back this year, Lewis?"

She smiled at me almost apologetically. She knew the reason as well as I did.

"We can't," I said. "There's not enough money."

"There's enough for our tickets."

I'd explained all that to her before, too. Perhaps she'd forgotten. Lately I often had to explain things more than once.

"You can't buy passage unless you have enough extra for insurance, and travelers' checks, and passport tax. The company has to protect itself. Unless you're financially responsible, they won't take you on the ships."

She shook her head. "Sometimes I wonder if we'll ever have enough."

We'd saved our money for years, but it was a pitifully small savings. We weren't rich people who could go down to the spaceport and buy passage on the rocket ships, no questions asked, no bond required. We were only farmers, eking our livelihood from the unproductive Martian soil, only two of the countless little people of the solar system. In all our lifetime we'd never been able to save enough to go home to Earth.

"One more year," I said. "If the crop prices stay up...."

She smiled, a sad little smile that didn't reach her eyes. "Yes, Lewis," she said. "One more year."

But I couldn't stop thinking of what she'd said earlier, nor stop seeing her thin, tired body. Neither of us was strong any more, but of the two I was far stronger than she.

When we'd left Earth she'd been as eager and graceful as a child. We hadn't been much past childhood then, either of us....

"Sometimes I wonder why we ever came here," she said.

"It's been a good life."

She sighed. "I know. But now that it's nearly over, there's nothing to hold us here."

"No," I said. "There's not."

If we had had children it might have been different. As it was, we lived surrounded by the children and grandchildren of our friends. Our friends themselves were dead. One by one they had died, all of those who came with us on the first colonizing ship to Mars. All of those who came later, on the second and third ships. Their children were our neighbors now—and they were Martian born. It wasn't the same.

She leaned over and pressed my hand. "We'd better go in, Lewis," she said. "We need our sleep."

Her eyes were raised again to the green star that was Earth. Watching her, I knew that I loved her now as much as when we had been young together. More, really, for we had added years of shared memories. I wanted so much to give her what she longed for, what we both longed for. But I couldn't think of any way to do it. Not this year.

Once, almost seventy years before, I had smiled at the girl who had just promised to become my wife, and I'd said: "I'll give you the world, darling. All tied up in pink ribbons."

I didn't want to think about that now.

We got up and went into the house and shut the veranda door behind us.

★ ★ ★

I couldn't go to sleep. For hours I lay in bed staring up at the shadowed ceiling, trying to think of some way to raise the money. But there wasn't any way that I could see. It would be at least eight months before enough of the greenhouse crops were harvested.

What would happen, I wondered, if I went to the spaceport and asked for tickets? If I explained that we couldn't buy insurance, that we couldn't put up the bond guaranteeing we wouldn't become public charges back on Earth…. But all the time I wondered I knew the answer. Rules were rules. They wouldn't be broken especially not for two old farmers who had long outlived their usefulness and their time.

Martha sighed in her sleep and turned over. It was light enough now for me to see her face clearly. She was smiling. But a minute ago she had been crying, for the tears were still wet on her cheeks.

Perhaps she was dreaming of Earth again.

Suddenly, watching her, I didn't care if they laughed at me or lectured me on my responsibilities to the government as if I were a senile fool. I was going to the spaceport. I was going to find out if, somehow, we couldn't go back.

I got up and dressed and went out, walking softly so as not to awaken her. But even so she heard me and called out to me.

"Lewis...."

I turned at the head of the stairs and looked back into the room.

"Don't get up, Martha," I said. "I'm going into town."

"All right, Lewis."

She relaxed, and a minute later she was asleep again. I tiptoed downstairs and out the front door to where the trike car was parked, and started for the village a mile to the west.

It was desert all the way. Dry, fine red sand that swirled upward in choking clouds, if you stepped off the pavement into it. The narrow road cut straight through it, linking the outlying district farms to the town. The farms themselves were planted in the desert. Small, glassed-in houses and barns, and large greenhouses roofed with even more glass that sheltered the Earth plants and gave them Earth air to breathe.

When I came to the second farmhouse John Emery hurried out to meet me.

"Morning, Lewis," he said. "Going to town?"

I shut off the motor and nodded. "I want to catch the early shuttle plane to the spaceport," I said. "I'm going to the city to buy some things."

I had to lie about it. I didn't want anyone to know we were even thinking of leaving, at least not until we had our tickets in our hands.

"Oh," Emery said. "That's right. I suppose you'll be buying Martha an anniversary present."

I stared at him blankly. I couldn't think what anniversary he meant.

"You'll have been here thirty-five years next week," he said. "That's a long time, Lewis...."

Thirty-five years. It took me a minute to realize what he meant. He was right. That was how long we had been here, in Martian years.

The others, those who had been born here on Mars, always used the Martian seasons. We had too, once. But lately we forgot, and counted in Earth time. It seemed more natural.

"Wait a minute, Lewis," Emery said. "I'll ride into the village with you. There's plenty of time for you to make your plane."

I went up on his veranda and sat down and waited for him to get ready. I leaned back in the swing chair and rocked slowly back and forth, wondering idly how many times I'd sat here.

This was old Tom Emery's house. Or had been, until he died eight years ago. He'd built this swing chair the very first year we'd been on Mars.

Now it was young John's. Young? That showed how old we were getting. John was sixty-three, in Earth years. He'd been born that second winter, the month the parasites got into the greenhouses.

He came back out onto the veranda. "Well, I'm ready, Lewis," he said.

We went down to my trike car and got in.

"You and Martha ought to get out more," he said. "Jenny's been asking me why you don't come to call."

I shrugged. I couldn't tell him we seldom went out because when we did we were always set apart and treated carefully, like children. He probably didn't even realize that it was so.

"Oh," I said. "We like it at home."

He smiled. "I suppose you do, after thirty-five years."

I started the motor quickly, and from then on concentrated on my driving. He didn't say anything more.

It took only a few minutes to get to the village, but even so I was tired. Lately it grew harder and harder to drive, to keep the trike car on the narrow strip of pavement. I was glad when we pulled up in the square and got out.

"I'll walk over to the plane with you," Emery said. "I've got plenty of time."

"All right."

"By the way, Lewis, Jenny and I and some of the neighbors thought we'd drop over on your anniversary."

"That's fine," I said, trying to sound enthusiastic. "Come on over."

"It's a big event," he said. "Deserves a celebration."

The shuttle plane was just landing. I hurried over to the ticket window, with him right beside me.

"I just wanted to be sure you'd be home," he said. "We wouldn't want you to miss your own party."

"Party?" I said. "But John—"

He wouldn't even let me finish protesting.

"Now don't ask any questions, Lewis. You wouldn't want to spoil the surprise, would you?"

He chuckled. "Your plane's loading now. You'd better be going. Thanks for the ride, Lewis."

I went across to the plane and got in. I hoped that somehow we wouldn't have to spend that Martian anniversary being congratulated and petted and babied. I didn't think Martha could stand it. But there wasn't any polite way to say no.

★ ★ ★

It wasn't a long trip to the spaceport. In less than an hour the plane dropped down to the air strip that flanked the rocket field. But it was like flying from one civilization to another.

The city was big, almost like an Earth city. There was lots of traffic, cars and copters and planes. All the bustle of the spaceways stations.

But although the city looked like Earth, it smelled as dry and alkaline as all the rest of Mars.

I found the ticket office easily enough and went in. The young clerk barely glanced up at me. "Yes?" he said.

"I want to inquire about tickets to Earth," I said.

My hands were sweating, and I could feel my heart pounding too fast against my ribs. But my voice sounded casual, just the way I wanted it to sound.

"Tickets?" the clerk said. "How many?"

"Two. How much would they cost? Everything included."

"Forty-two eighty," he said. His voice was still bored. "I could give them to you for the flight after next. Tourist class, of course."

We didn't have that much. We were at least three hundred short.

"Isn't there any way," I said hesitantly, "that I could get them for less? I mean, we wouldn't need insurance, would we?"

He looked up at me for the first time, startled. "You don't mean you want them for yourself, do you?"

"Why yes. For me and my wife."

He shook his head. "I'm sorry," he said flatly. "But that would be impossible in any case. You're too old."

He turned away from me and bent over his desk work again.

The words hung in the air. Too old… too old… I clutched the edge of the desk and steadied myself and forced down the panic I could feel rising.

"Do you mean," I said slowly, "that you wouldn't sell us tickets even if we had the money?"

He glanced up again, obviously annoyed at my persistence. "That's right. No passengers over seventy carried without special visas. Medical precaution."

I just stood there. This couldn't be happening. Not after all our years of working and saving and planning for the future. Not go back. Not even next year. Stay here, because we were old and frail and the ships wouldn't be bothered with us anyway.

Martha. How could I tell her? How could I say, "We can't go home, Martha. They won't let us."

I couldn't say it. There had to be some other way.

"Pardon me," I said to the clerk, "but who should I see about getting a visa?"

He swept the stack of papers away with an impatient gesture and frowned up at me.

"Over at the colonial office, I suppose," he said. "But it won't do you any good."

I could read in his eyes what he thought of me. Of me and all the other farmers who lived in the outlying districts and raised crops and seldom came to the city. My clothes were old and provincial and out of style, and so was I, to him.

"I'll try it anyway," I said.

He started to say something, then bit it back and looked away from me again. I was keeping him from his work. I was just a rude old man interfering with the operation of the spaceways.

Slowly I let go of the desk and turned to leave. It was hard to walk. My knees were trembling, and my whole body shook. It was all I could do not to cry. It angered me, the quavering in my voice and the weakness in my legs.

I went out into the hall and looked for the directory that would point the way to the colonial office. It wasn't far off.

I walked out onto the edge of the field and past the Earth rocket, its silver nose pointed up at the sky. I couldn't bear to look at it for longer than a minute.

It was only a few hundred yards to the colonial office, but it seemed like miles.

★ ★ ★

This office was larger than the other, and much more comfortable. The man seated behind the desk seemed friendlier too.

"May I help you?" he asked.

"Yes," I said slowly. "The man at the ticket office told me to come here. I wanted to see about getting a permit to go back to Earth."

His smile faded. "For yourself?"

"Yes," I said woodenly. "For myself and my wife."

"Well, Mr...."

"Farwell. Lewis Farwell."

"My name's Duane. Please sit down, won't you? How old are you, Mr. Farwell?"

"Eighty-seven," I said. "In Earth years."

He frowned. "The regulations say no space travel for people past seventy, except in certain special cases."

I looked down at my hands. They were shaking badly. I knew he could see them shake, and was judging me as old and weak and unable to stand the trip. He couldn't know why I was trembling.

"Please," I whispered. "It wouldn't matter if it hurt us. It's just that we want to see Earth again. It's been so long...."

"How long have you been here, Mr. Farwell?" It was merely politeness. There wasn't any promise in his voice.

"Sixty-five years." I looked up at him. "Isn't there some way—"

"Sixty-five years? But that means you must have come here on the first colonizing ship."

"Yes," I said. "We did."

"I can't believe it," he said slowly. "I can't believe I'm actually looking at one of the pioneers." He shook his head. "I didn't even know any of them were still on Mars."

"We're the last ones," I said. "That's the main reason we want to go back. It's awfully hard staying on when your friends are dead."

Duane got up and crossed the room to the window and looked out over the rocket field.

"But what good would it do to go back, Mr. Farwell?" he asked. "Earth has changed very much in the last sixty-five years."

He was trying to soften the disappointment. But nothing could. If only I could make him realize that.

"I know it's changed," I said. "But it's *home*. Don't you see? We're Earthmen still. I guess that never changes. And now that we're old, we're aliens here."

"We're all aliens here, Mr. Farwell."

"No," I said desperately. "Maybe you are. Maybe a lot of the city people are. But our neighbors were born on Mars. To them Earth is a legend. A place where their ancestors once lived. It's not real to them."

He turned and crossed the room and came back to me. His smile was pitying. "If you went back," he said, "you'd find you were a Martian, too."

I couldn't reach him. He was friendly and pleasant and he was trying to make things easier, and it wasn't any use talking. I bent my head and choked back the sobs I could feel rising in my throat.

"You've lived a full life," Duane said. "You were one of the pioneers. I remember reading about your ship when I was a boy, and wishing I'd been born sooner so that I could have been on it."

Slowly I raised my head and looked up at him.

"Please," I said. "I know that. I'm glad we came here. If we had our lives to live over, we'd come again. We'd go through all the hardships of those first few years, and enjoy them just as much. We'd be just as thrilled over proving that it's possible to farm a world like this, where it's always freezing and the air is thin and nothing will grow outside the greenhouses. You don't need to tell me what we've done, or what we've gotten out of it. We know. We've had a wonderful life here."

"But you still want to go back?"

"Yes," I said. "We still want to go back. We're tired of living in the past, with our friends dead and nothing to do except remember."

He looked at me for a long moment. Then he said slowly, "You realize, don't you, that if you went back to Earth you'd have to stay there? You couldn't return to Mars."

"I realize that," I said. "That's what we want. We want to die at home. On Earth."

For a long, long moment his eyes never left mine. Then, slowly, he sat down at his desk and reached for a pen.

"All right, Mr. Farwell," he said. "I'll give you a visa."

I couldn't believe it. I stared at him, sure that I'd misunderstood.

"Sixty-five years...." He shook his head. "I only hope I'm doing the right thing. I hope you won't regret this."

"We won't," I whispered.

Then I remembered that we were still short of money. That that was why I'd come to the spaceport originally. I was almost afraid to mention it, for fear I'd lose everything.

"Is there—is there some way we could be excused from the insurance?" I said. "So we could go back this year? We're three hundred short."

He smiled. It was a very reassuring smile. "You don't need to worry about the money," he said. "The colonial office can take care of that. After all, we owe your generation a great debt, Mr. Farwell. A passport tax and the fare to Earth are little enough to pay for a planet."

I didn't quite understand him, but that didn't matter. The only thing that mattered was that we were going home. Back to Earth. I could see Martha's face when I told her. I could see her tears of happiness.

There were tears on my own cheeks, but I wasn't ashamed of them now.

"Mr. Farwell," Duane said. "You go back home. The shuttle ship will be leaving in a few minutes."

"You mean that—" I started.

He nodded. "I'll get your tickets for you. On the first ship I can. Just leave it to me."

"It's too much trouble," I protested.

"No it's not." He smiled. "Besides, I'd like to bring them out to you. I'd like to see your farm, if I may."

Then I remembered what John Emery had said this morning about our anniversary. It would be a wonderful celebration, now that there was something to celebrate. We could even save our announcement that we were going home until then.

"Mr. Duane," I said. "Next week, on the tenth, we'll have been here thirty-five Martian years. Maybe you'd like to come out then. I guess our neighbors will be giving us a sort of party."

He laid the pen down and looked at me very intently. "They don't know you're planning to leave yet, do they?"

"No. We'll wait and tell them then."

Duane nodded slowly. "I'll be there," he promised.

★ ★ ★

Martha was out on the veranda again, looking down the road toward the village. All afternoon at least one of us had been out there watching for our guests, waiting for our anniversary celebration to begin.

"Do you see anyone yet?" I called.

"No," she said. "Not yet."

I looked around the room hoping I'd find something left undone that I could work on, so I wouldn't have to sit and worry about the possibility of Duane's having forgotten us. But everything was ready. The extra chairs were out and the furniture all dusted, and Martha's cakes and cookies arranged on the table.

I couldn't sit still. Not today. I got up out of the chair and joined her on the veranda.

"I wonder what their surprise is," she said. "Didn't John give you any hint at all?"

"No," I said. "But whatever it is, it can't be half as wonderful as ours."

She reached for my hand. "Lewis," she whispered. "I can hardly believe it, can you?"

"No," I said. "But it's true. We're really going."

I put my arm around her, and she rested her head against me.

"I'm so happy, Lewis."

Her cheeks were full of color once again, and her step had a spring to it that I hadn't seen for years. It was as if the years of waiting were falling away from both of us now.

"I wish they'd come," she said. "I can hardly wait to see their faces when we tell them."

It was getting late in the afternoon. Already the sun was dipping down toward the desert horizon. It was hard to wait. In some ways it was harder to be patient these last few hours than it had been during all those years we'd wanted to go back.

"Look," Martha said suddenly. "There's a car now."

Then I saw the car too, coming quickly toward us. It pulled up in front of the house and stopped and Duane stepped out.

"Well, hello there, Mr. Farwell," he called. "All ready for the trip?"

I nodded. Suddenly, now that he was here, I couldn't say anything at all.

He must have seen how excited we were. By the time he was inside the veranda door he'd reached into his wallet and pulled out a long envelope.

"Here's your schedule," he said. "Your tickets are all made out for next week's flight."

Martha's hand crept into mine. "You've been so kind," she whispered.

We went into the house and smiled at each other while Duane admired the furniture and the farming district in general and our place in particular. We hardly heard what he was saying.

When the doorbell rang we stared at each other. For a minute I couldn't think who it might be. I'd forgotten our guests and their surprise party, even the anniversary itself had slipped my mind.

"Hello in there," John Emery called. "Come on out, you two."

Martha pressed my hand once more. Then she stepped to the door and opened it.

"Happy anniversary!"

We stood frozen. We'd expected only a few visitors, some of our nearest neighbors. But the yard was full of people. They crowded up our walk and in the road and more of them were still piling out of cars. It looked as if everyone in the district was along.

"Come on out," Emery called. "You too, Duane."

The two men smiled at each other knowingly, and for just a moment I had time to wonder why.

Then Martha clutched my arm. "You tell him, Lewis."

"John," I said. "We have a surprise for you too—"

He wouldn't let me finish. He took hold of my arm with one hand and Martha's with the other and drew us outside where everyone could see us.

"You can tell us later, Lewis," he said, "First we have a surprise for you!"

"But wait—"

They crowded in around us, laughing and waving and calling "Happy anniversary". We couldn't resist them. They swept us along with them down the walk and into one of the cars.

I looked around for Duane. He was in the back seat, smiling somewhat nervously. Perhaps he thought that this was normal farm life.

"Lewis," Martha said, "where are they taking us?"

"I don't know...."

The cars started, ours leading the way. It was a regular procession back to the village, with everyone laughing and calling to us and telling us how happy we were going to be with our surprise. Every time we tried to ask questions, John Emery interrupted.

"Just wait and see," he kept saying. "Wait and see."

At the end of the village square they'd put up a platform. It wasn't very big, nor very well made, but it was strung with yards of bunting and a huge sign that said, "Happy Anniversary, Lewis and Martha."

We were pushed toward it, carried along by the swarm of people. There wasn't any way to resist. Martha clung to my arm, pressing close against me. She was trembling again.

"What does it mean, Lewis?"

"I wish I knew."

They pushed us right up onto the platform and John Emery followed us up and held out his hand to quiet the crowd. I put my arm around Martha and looked down at them. Hundreds of people. All in their best clothes. Our friends' children and grandchildren, and even great-grandchildren.

"I won't make a speech," John Emery said when they were finally quiet. "You know why we're here today—all of you except Lewis and Martha know. It's an anniversary. A big anniversary. Thirty-five years today since our fathers—and you two—landed here on Mars."

He paused. He didn't seem to know what to say next. Finally he turned and swept his arm past the platform to where a big canvas-covered object stood on the ground.

"Unveil it," he said.

The crowd grew absolutely quiet. A couple of boys stepped up and pulled the canvas off.

"There's your surprise," John Emery said softly.

It was a statue. A life-size statue carved from the dull red stone of Mars. Two figures, a man and a woman, dressed in farm clothes, standing side by side and looking out across the square toward the open desert.

They were very real, those figures. Real, and somehow familiar.

"Lewis," Martha whispered. "They're—they're us!"

She was right. It was a statue of us. Neither old nor young, but ageless. Two farmers, looking out forever across the endless Martian desert.

There was an inscription on the base, but I couldn't quite make it out. Martha could. She read it, slowly, while everyone in the crowd stood silent, listening.

"Lewis and Martha Farwell," she read. "The last of the pioneers—" Her voice broke. "Underneath," she whispered, "it says—the first Martians. And then it lists them—us."

She read the list, all the names of our friends who had come out on that first ship. The names of men and women who had died, one by one, and left their farms to their children—to the same children who now crowded close about the platform and listened to her read, and smiled up at us.

She came to the end of the list and looked out at the crowd. "Thank you," she whispered.

They shouted then. They called out to us and pressed forward and held their babies up to see us.

I looked out past the people, across the flat red desert to the horizon, toward the spot in the east where the Earth would rise, much later. The dry smell of Mars had never been stronger.

The first Martians....

They were so real, those carved figures. Lewis and Martha Farwell.

"Look at them, Lewis," Martha said softly. "They're cheering us. Us!"

She was smiling. There were tears in her eyes, but her smile was bright and proud and shining. Slowly she turned away from me and straightened, staring out over the heads of the crowd across the desert to the east. She stood with her head thrown back and her mouth smiling, and she was as proudly erect as the statue that was her likeness.

"Martha," I whispered. "How can we tell them goodbye?"

Then she turned to face me, and I could see the tears glistening in her eyes. "We can't leave, Lewis. Not after this."

She was right, of course. We couldn't leave. We were symbols. The last of the pioneers. The first Martians. And they had carved their symbol in our image and made us a part of Mars forever.

I glanced down, along the rows of upturned, laughing faces, searching for Duane. He was easy to find. He was the only one who wasn't shouting. His eyes met mine, and I didn't have to say anything. He knew. He climbed up beside me on the platform.

I tried to speak, but I couldn't.

"Tell him, Lewis," Martha whispered. "Tell him we can't go."

Then she was crying. Her smile was gone and her proud look was gone and her hand crept into mine and trembled there. I put my arm around her shoulders, but there was no way I could comfort her.

"Now we'll never go," she sobbed. "We'll never get home."

I don't think I had ever realized, until that moment, just how much it meant to her—getting home. Much more, perhaps, than it had ever meant to me.

The statues were only statues. They were carved from the stone of Mars. And Martha wanted Earth. We both wanted Earth. Home.

I looked away from her then, back to Duane. "No," I said. "We're still going. Only—" I broke off, hearing the shouting and the cheers and the children's laughter. "Only, how can we tell *them*?"

Duane smiled. "Don't try to, Mr. Farwell," he said softly. "Just wait and see."

He turned, nodded to where John Emery still stood at the edge of the platform. "All right, John."

Emery nodded too, and then he raised his hand. As he did so, the shouting stopped and the people stood suddenly quiet, still looking up at us.

"You all know that this is an anniversary," John Emery said. "And you all know something else that Lewis and Martha thought they'd kept as a surprise—that this is more than an anniversary. It's goodbye."

I stared at him. He knew. All of them knew. And then I looked at Duane and saw that he was smiling more than ever.

"They've lived here on Mars for thirty-five years," John Emery said. "And now they're going back to Earth."

Martha's hand tightened on mine. "Look, Lewis," she cried. "Look at them. They're not angry. They're—they're happy for us!"

John Emery turned to face us. "Surprised?" he said.

I nodded. Martha nodded too. Behind him, the people cheered again.

"I thought you would be," Emery said. Then, "I'm not very good at speeches, but I just wanted you to know how much we've enjoyed being your neighbors. Don't forget us when you get back to Earth."

★ ★ ★

It was a long, long trip from Mars to Earth. Three months on the ship, thirty-five million miles. A trip we had dreamed about for so long, without any real hope of ever making it. But now it was over. We were back on Earth. Back where we had started from.

"It's good to be alone, isn't it, Lewis?" Martha leaned back in her chair and smiled up at me.

I nodded. It did feel good to be here in the apartment, just the two of us, away from the crowds and the speeches and the official welcomes and the flashbulbs popping.

"I wish they wouldn't make such a fuss over us," she said. "I wish they'd leave us alone."

"You can't blame them," I said, although I couldn't help wishing the same thing. "We're celebrities. What was it that reporter said about us? That we're part of history."

She sighed. She turned away from me and looked out the window again, past the buildings and the lighted traffic ramps and the throngs of people bustling by outside, people who couldn't see in through the one-way glass, people whom we couldn't hear because the room was soundproofed.

"Mars should be up by now," she said.

"It probably is." I looked out again, although I knew that we would see nothing. No stars. No planets. Not even the moon, except as a pale half disc peering through the haze. The lights from the city were too bright. The air held the light and reflected it down again, and the sky was a deep, dark blue with the buildings about us towering into it, outlined blackly against it. And we couldn't see the stars.

"Lewis," Martha said slowly. "I never thought it would have changed this much, did you?"

"No." I couldn't tell from her voice whether she liked the changes or not. Lately I couldn't tell much of anything from her voice. And nothing was the same as we had remembered it.

Even the Earth farms were mechanized now. Factory production lines for food, as well as for everything else. It was necessary, of course. We had heard all the reasons, all the theories, all the latest statistics.

"I guess I'll go to bed soon," Martha said. "I'm tired."

"It's the higher gravity." We'd both been tired since we got back to Earth. We had forgotten, over the years, what Earth gravity was like.

She hesitated. She smiled at me, but her eyes were worried. "Lewis—are you really glad we came back?"

It was the first time she had asked me that. And there was only one answer I could give her. The one she expected.

"Of course, Martha."

She sighed again. She got up out of the chair and turned toward the bedroom door, and then she paused there by the window looking out at the deep blue sky.

"Are you really glad, Lewis?"

Then I knew. Or, at least, I hoped. "Why, Martha? Aren't you?"

For one long minute she stood beside me, looking up at the Mars we couldn't see. And then she turned to face me once again, and I could see the tears.

"Oh, Lewis, I want to go home!"

Full circle. We had both come full circle these last few hectic weeks on Earth.

"So do I, Martha."

"Do you, Lewis?" And then the tiredness came back to her eyes and she looked away again. "But of course we can't."

Slowly I crossed over to the desk and opened the top drawer and took out the folder that Duane had given me, that last day at the spaceport, just before our ship to Earth had blasted off. Slowly I unfolded the paper that Duane had told me to keep in case we ever wanted it.

"Yes, we can, Martha. We can go back."

"What's that, Lewis?" And then she saw what it was. Her face came alive again, and her eyes were shining. "We're going home?" she whispered. "We're really going home?"

I looked down at the Earth–Mars half of the round trip ticket that Duane had given me, and I knew that this time she was right.

This time we'd really be going home.

The Old Martians

by Rog Phillips

The man with the pith helmet had his back toward me. Hunched forward, he was screaming at the girl in the lens of his camera. "Don't just stand there, Dotty! Move! Do something! Back up toward that column with inscriptions on it."

The girl was tall and long-legged with ideal body proportions, her features and skin coloring a perfect norm-blend with no throwback elements. Right now she seemed confused and half-frightened as she tried to comply with the directions of the man with the movie camera. She smiled artificially, turned her head to look at the fragment of a wall behind her, reached out with a finger and started tracing the lines of an almost obliterated inscription in its stone surface.

The camera stopped whirring. Its owner straightened and grumbled, "That's all."

Now the girl was allowed to go back to her worrying. Swiftly she surveyed the crowd, but didn't find the person she was looking for. She started moving toward one of the arches that led deeper into the ruins.

I followed her slowly.

She passed through the arch, stopped, and turned her head toward the right, her eyes on something out of sight. She'd found him, but she saw me at the same time and her worry deepened.

When she moved back into the crowd, I strolled casually through the archway.

There was a vaguely defined passageway, the roof over it gone for half a million years, of course. And twenty feet away, oblivious of his surroundings except for what was directly in front of him, was my man.

His height and build were somewhat less than the norm. But it was his profile that drew my attention. A remarkable throwback; a throwback of a distinct type.

In fact, he might well have served as the model in the types textbooks labeled British. The resemblance was subtle. Only one trained to differentiate would ever have noticed it.

I let my attention take in his whole figure. His elbows had a habit of making fluttery movements when his exploring hands paused so that a strange birdlike impression was given. Also an air of ungainliness in the lines of the lean body, rather than the feline smoothness and grace of the norm-blend. It was so in keeping with his features that it served to strengthen the psycho diagnosis.

A throwback to an era ten thousand years in the past, and therefore, as the textbooks say, prone to mental instability. It was no wonder that the girl called Dotty had had the air of being perpetually worried!

She appeared now, from the far side of the ruin and approached the man.

He sensed rather than saw her and straightened up, every line of him etched with excitement.

"Dotty!" he said. "I've found it. I've found the proof. I've been here before, thousands of years ago when this wasn't ruins. I *remember*."

The girl's manner reflected weariness, "Please, Herb. You've got to forget all about it. You'll talk too much!"

His shoulders stiffened. "Don't worry. I won't talk until I have proof to convince even them. Somewhere around here something lies buried. Something I will be able to remember. They will dig where the rocks haven't been touched for five thousand centuries and find what I say is there."

Dotty was shaking her head. "No, Herb. If it were on Earth I might half believe you. But not here on Mars. These—these people weren't even humanoid!"

"*Neither was I*," Herb whispered hoarsely.

I sighed regretfully. I'd seen too many cases like this one. I'd grown to dread them. But it was a job and a man had to eat.

The guide began herding the tourists back to the bus. I mingled with the crowd, and when Dotty and Herb climbed aboard I managed to stick close to them.

"Where'd you two go to?" the man in the pith helmet called from where he was sitting. "Stick close to me. I put a new roll in the camera. At the next place I want to get some shots of both of you together."

"All right, George," Dotty said obediently.

She and Herb were forced to find separate seats. They would do no talking, so I faced around and studied the three alternately. The man in the pith helmet, George, was a normal blend; totally unconcerned about his reactions on others so long as he could pursue his hobby.

The bus detoured a roped-off area in the center of the ancient city, the part considered too dangerous because of cave-in possibilities, and made its way out to the northern edge of ruins to the part that resembled the ancient cemeteries on Earth. The only major difference was that there were no remains under the evenly spaced stones. There was some doubt that it had been a cemetery. But the guide announced it as one. And that announcement as the bus came to a stop had a pronounced effect on Herb. He began his fluttery elbow movements again and looked around at Dotty with a triumphant smile. I moved up quickly to keep him in earshot.

He protested when George insisted on taking camera shots, then gave in and cooperated in order to get it over with.

Finally George snapped his camera shut. Herb mumbled something to Dotty that I didn't catch, and started down one of the lanes between rows of stones as though headed for a definite goal.

I couldn't very well follow after they left the main group. It would have been obvious. Instead, I veered off to one side, gambling that when they reached their destination I would be able to read their lips.

I got well away from stragglers and took out my mirroscope, pointing if off in the distance and swinging the objective lens around until it centered on them. I was lucky. They were facing in my direction.

"It isn't a cemetery," Herb was saying with emphatic motions of his hands. "It was a parking area, and this stone was where I parked my airsled. I can remember it as though it were yesterday."

I had to admire the man's subconscious. It was a remarkably shrewd guess. The experts wouldn't play along with it, but they would probably never be able to prove him wrong on that count. But Dotty was arguing with him. "How can you prove it was a parking area?" Her eyes roamed over the large field with its regularly spaced stones. "It certainly looks impractical for a parking lot."

"Just the same, that's what it was. I wish I had a shovel here. I seem to remember burying something near my stone. If I could find that it would prove I really remember."

"Why don't you forget it?" Dotty pleaded. "After all, even if it were true, what does it matter *now*?"

"It matters to me. Ever since we arrived here I've seen familiar things. Too familiar to be coincidence. I never felt this way before. I always considered reincarnation as ancient superstitious belief, just like everyone else. But not now. I *know*. I lived here when all this was new."

"But can't you just be satisfied to feel that you did and let it go at that?" Dotty asked. "I'm afraid of what they would do to you if they found out what you're thinking."

"Hah!" Herb snorted. "I have a feeling that before we leave Mars I'll be able to prove it to them. Somewhere in this city is something that only I know exists. It's hidden under stones that haven't been disturbed since man first set foot on the planet. It isn't entirely clear yet, but it will come—it will come. Then I'll make them listen. They'll dig, and they'll find what I say is there. You wait and see."

"They'll lock you up, darling," Dotty said. "They won't believe you."

The guide was calling everyone back to the bus. I watched Herb scowl fiercely at the stone marker that he believed to have been his, open his mouth to say something, then turn away so that his lips were out of sight. Regretfully I put the mirroscope away and went back to the bus.

I knew where we were going next, and I was uneasy about it. Herb and Dotty managed to sit together and I got a place right behind them where I could eavesdrop. But they sat in silence.

The bus had left the ancient city behind, to head out over the desert toward one of the few structures on Mars which had withstood the ravages of time without crumbling. An immense dome of solid concrete reinforced with pure copper rods harder than steel. The Martians had known what Earth civilization didn't learn until around the year three thousand: that copper can't be tempered, but pure copper becomes tempered of itself in a thousand years.

That immense dome was a honeycomb of passageways and rooms, some of which were not open to tourists. It would be a natural for Herb.

The bus stopped. The people were piling out and staring curiously at the smooth surface of the dome. Especially at places where the reinforcement rods were protruding and glittering like tarnished gold.

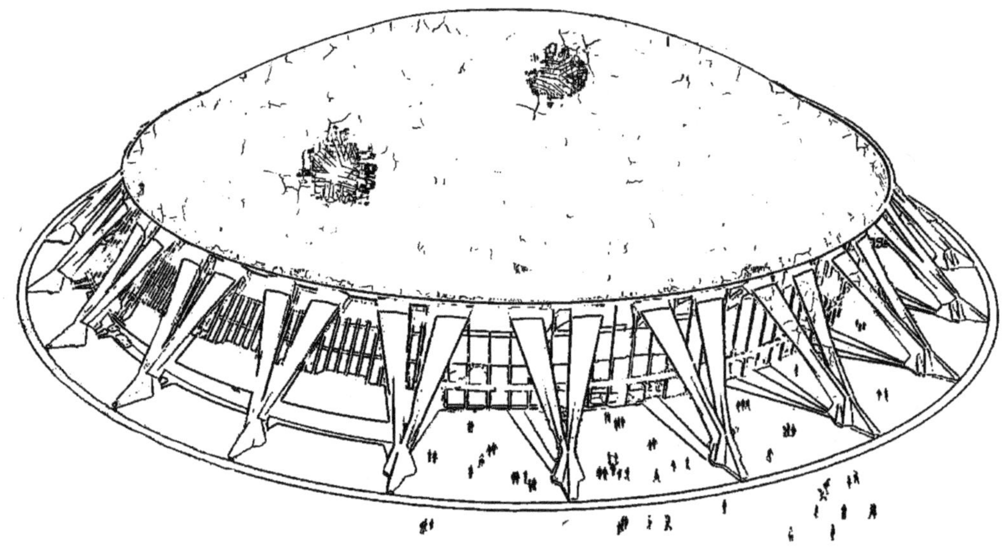

Two of the permanent guards had come out to take charge of the tour. I caught the eye of one of them and nodded toward Herb. The guard caught my meaning, edged over to his partner, and soon both men were warned that Herb was to be closely watched.

I felt better, knowing that a couple of others knew about him. Maybe it would have been smarter to have taken him in custody right then. But it would have meant a scene.

The procedure of the tour was for the guide to do all the talking, leading the procession through the roped off parts of the dome, while the two guards followed along behind to make sure no stragglers got left.

I let three or four people move in front of me so Herb wouldn't get suspicious. Dotty was sticking close to him, plainly worried. And he was more excited than he had been at any of the other spots. He fairly quivered, his eyes caressing the walls with a fevered look.

Dotty didn't miss his increased agitation. Especially after he whispered in her ear a couple of times.

The guide took the usual path. Straight into the dome, pausing at half a dozen small rooms with carved walls, to arrive at a bank of elevators installed in the exact center; then straight up to the roof and the observation platform from which miles and miles of desert and ruins could be seen. Then back down to the second level, a zig-zag course through other rooms, and finally down a flight of steps to where the tour started.

I kept my eyes on the back of Herb's head. You can tell a lot by doing that. At first his head turned this way and that, indicating he was full of curiosity. I was waiting for that telltale sudden tensing, with the head directed at some spot, which would tell of a sudden "memory" stirring in the man's mind.

I almost missed it when it came, because it was between two passages—a blank wall. The briefest pause, then Herb was going on again as though nothing had happened.

But now his head had stopped its curiosity-motivated pivoting. It was the head of a man who was no longer curious—who has made up his mind about something. I didn't like it.

And when the group emerged into open air once more without Herb having tried anything I knew as certainly as I had ever known anything that he intended coming back here, and soon.

In the comfort station before boarding the bus I scrawled a hasty note to the guards to investigate the spot halfway between passageways 14 and 15 on the first level, and slipped it to one of them as I passed him to get on the bus.

We visited four other spots on the tour. When Herb showed no real interest in them it only clinched what I was already sure of, that he planned on returning.

★ ★ ★

At the Ancient City Hotel once again, I gave the high sign, and shortly Herb and Dotty were being watched by capable men, leaving me free to go to my room.

Once there, I called the dome. They were just getting the X-ray setup in place to explore that wall and promised to call me as soon as they were finished. Next I called C.I. and made my report. I was still making it when the operator broke in.

"Steve Merrit wants to talk to you," she said crisply.

"Make the circuit three way," I said.

Steve's voice came in. "I had to get to you, Joe. This guy Herb and his wife just left the hotel."

"C.I.'s listening too," I said. "Did they say anything that would point to where they're going?"

"To the cemetery first. He swiped a couple of knives and forks when they finished eating their dinner. Maybe for weapons."

"I doubt that," I said. "But I think it's time to pick him up. He's got to be committed."

"Wait a minute," C.I. said. "Joe, you catch up with them. Join them and play along. Tell this guy Herb you overheard him and guessed what was going on. Gain his confidence if you can."

"That's pretty dangerous!" I replied. "That guy's—"

"It's orders," C.I. said. "Steve, you lay the net so that whatever happens we can contain it."

That was that. Orders. But I still didn't like it.

I went to the desk and took out my compact paralysis tube. Then, reluctantly, I put it back. I would have to play the part. The paralysis tube would give me away as an agent. It would have to be up to Steve and the others to contain the threat.

Down in the lobby I saw Steve waiting impatiently. He was uneasy, too. "What's come over C.I.? They're toying with dynamite on this."

"I think I know what they want, they want to let him go far enough so we can see more of the nature of the danger. And I hope nobody gets killed. They should have spotted this Herb guy and not let him come here at all. I suspect they did spot him, and let him come to conduct another of their damned experiments. They don't want to leave well enough alone."

We were outside now. No one was around. The sun was just beginning to set, and the instant it disappeared the night would be pitch-black. Even if one of the moons was out.

"We'll be watching on the standard C.I. band," Steve assured me. "They're at the temple right now, waiting for it to get dark." He grinned. "Good luck." There was a mixture of genuineness, half mockery, and worry in his voice.

At the temple ruins I found them easily enough and took the simplest course. I walked right up to them.

"Hello," I said. "I thought I'd find you here. I want to go along with you. I'm interested."

"What do you mean?" Herb was hostile and suspicious.

"You remember me. I was on the tour this afternoon. I accidentally overheard you. It would *be* something if reincarnation could be proven."

"Do you believe in reincarnation?"

I frowned as though being cautious. "I don't know." Then I put a disarming grin on my lips. "Since believing in it is legally classified as insanity, for the records, no." It was a nice statement. It could imply that I did, and Herb took that implication. He accepted me. Dotty was different.

"How do you know he isn't an agent?" she asked Herb uneasily.

"If I am, the fat's in the fire," I told her. "But wouldn't I be locking him up?" This quieted, but didn't satisfy her. "Anyway," I said, "if you can dig up something that you remember burying, an extra witness won't do any harm. That's what you're after, isn't it? Proof that will end the last bit of doubt?"

"That's right," Herb said. "And you can help me dig."

"Okay then," I said. And it was settled. We introduced ourselves, then lapsed into silence while we waited for the sun to set. It wasn't long.

★ ★ ★

The place looked more like a cemetery than ever in the eerie glow of black light pencils as we made our way along a row of stone markers. Herb strode purposefully. Dotty stuck close to him, still a little suspicious of me. I trailed half a step behind.

Finally Herb stopped beside one of the markers. "This is it," he said softly. I blinked at the marker, then at Herb. It wasn't the one he had singled out in the afternoon. Was he mixed up?

If he wasn't he was a good actor. He took out one of the dinner knives and squatted down and started to probe the soil, loosening it so that it could be scraped out by hand.

I watched him dig. Part of the time I helped him. We found nothing. After a reasonable amount of this Herb stood up with a resigned sigh. "Guess I was wrong," he said.

"Poor Herby," Dotty said.

"Yeah, poor Herby," Herb said with every appearance of tiredness and defeat. "But—that's that. Sorry to have gotten you all excited about nothing, Joe. Guess it was too much to expect anything." He turned to Dotty. "As long as we're out here, let's take a walk by ourselves. Huh?"

That was as obvious a cue as I had ever been handed. Neat. I was confronted with the alternatives of scramming or calling him a liar.

"Guess I might as well go back to the hotel," I said cheerfully. "See you in the morning."

I headed back the way we had come until I was sure they couldn't hear me or see me with their black light pencils. Then, ducking down next to a marker I waited. After a couple of minutes I heard cautious footsteps.

"It's me, Joe—Steve."

"Good," I grunted. "What are they doing now? They gave me the brush-off."

"I got the play," Steve said. "Slick. Should we close in now, or wait?"

"I think I'll play my part a little further. Don't want C.I. to think we're timid."

"Okay," Steve said. "The next funeral we attend may be our own."

"Yeah," I said. "It might."

I moved into the darkness, not using my black light pencil, but keeping my sensitized glasses on so I could see Herb's if I got close enough.

I reached the spot where we had done the digging. I hesitated, then kept on, toward the spot where Herb and Dotty had been so engrossed that afternoon. In my mind's eye I knew exactly where it was.

My hands explored ahead of me, searching out each stone marker along my path, clinging to it as I passed it, and slipping off as I went on to the next. They were my only contact with reality in this total blackness.

I was thinking, too. I was thinking of what Herb had said about this being a parking area for airsleds back before the earliest known records of man on Earth when this city was alive. He was probably right about it at that. Analysis had shown the presence of copper and aluminum in the top surface of some of the markers that could only be accounted for by some metallic object setting atop each one long ago, and remaining so that molecular and atomic creep could set in, carrying such atoms deep into the surface crystals of the stone.

And I was wondering what it was he hoped to dig up. If it were some sort of weapon it probably wouldn't work after all this time. It couldn't! Or could it? A few things had been pieced together about the ancient Martian civilization. Not much, but enough to be sure that they knew a few things we had never discovered. They had been masters at creating machines with no moving parts. The electronic devices we had found had proven they knew far more about V.H.F. than we did.

I could see what C.I. was aiming at now. We might not even recognize what Herb was searching for. It would be better to let him find it, and get it from him before he could use it. If it was a weapon.

And it probably was a weapon. I was pretty sure his main objective was hidden in the wall in the dome, and that this thing in the cemetery was something that would help him get to that objective.

My thoughts came back to my surroundings. I was less than a dozen feet from where Herb and Dotty should be. I stopped. There was no trace of black light. I held my breath and listened. And I heard the faint scraping of the knife against stone.

I wished fervently that I had a standard C.I. infrascope so that I could see. Steve probably knew more of what was going on than I did. I had counted on watching Herb by his own black light pencil, and he was working in darkness.

Carefully I stole forward, inch by slow inch, my ears tuned for the faintest significant sound such as a grunt of satisfaction that would tell of finding what he was digging for.

And a million thoughts taunted me, thoughts about the latest discoveries in disintegration frequencies, thoughts about how little we knew of that ancient Martian civilization.

But also I was figuring what Herb would do. He would find the object he was digging for. Unwittingly he would grunt his triumph. Dotty might forget his strict warnings to be quiet, and say something. Regardless of that, he would stand up slowly, fondling what he had found, remembering what it was and how it worked. There would be a few seconds before it would become a weapon in his hands, seconds that I had to make the most use of, and be ready for.

"Uh!" It was the triumphant grunt I had known would come.

Sudden panic made me cast aside whatever vague plan of action I had had.

I turned on my pencil, bathing the two in its black light. At the same time I said, "I *thought* it was a scheme to get rid of me."

It was the element of surprise that saved me. A still picture of the scene the black light disclosed etched itself into my mind. There was an object in Herb's hand. A strange, meaningless object, dirty, yet with definite form. It was cradled in his hand like a weapon. It was pointed almost at me.

I dropped my pencil and went in low, diving for his legs. I felt the air crackle where I had just stood. As my arms encircled his legs I heard thunder exploding nearby.

Training has its advantages. The moment I felt contact with Herb that training took over. I jerked and rolled in a movement calculated to throw him to the ground face down, the motion ending in a backbreaker hold.

But only a part of my mind was concerned with that. The other part was frozen with horror. Approximately a half acre of the cemetery was glowing. I saw Steve in the center of it with Herb's weapon pointing his way. The very inertia of matter held Steve together for that brief instant, then he was falling apart, melting and evaporating at the same time, just like the stone markers and the ground around him.

I had the thing away from him suddenly, and I wondered what to do next. Running footsteps gave me the answer. It was other C.I. agents closing in.

Seconds later they had Herb under control. Dotty was wringing her hands and crying.

Me, I was holding the thing, afraid to let go of it and afraid to keep on holding it. But as the seconds passed without it exploding into destructive action again I began to let myself think I might live a while longer.

The area of destruction was molten now. Its heat was like that of an open blast furnace.

We skirted it and headed toward the road, lights in the distance telling us that cars were on the way to get us.

I saw Dotty stumble. I took her arm. She looked up at me, recognized me in the light from the glowing pool of bubbling lava, and tried to pull away.

"Take it easy," I said gruffly. "I'm your friend. Maybe the only friend you've got here."

Her look told me she didn't believe me, but she didn't pull away any more.

We walked along, and after a moment she seemed to struggle up out of her mental paralysis.

"Herb was right!" she said in a low, wondering tone. "He really did remember."

"It was plain coincidence," I said sharply, "and don't ever let yourself think differently. He's insane. It's a recognized form of insanity. He'll be sent to a good mental hospital, and in a year or two he'll come out good as new."

"Coincidence?" she echoed. Then she laughed. It was mirth that drifted quickly into hysterical hopelessness. I dug my fingers into her flesh until the pain brought her to her senses.

"Coincidence," I said. "Nothing more. I've seen seventeen cases just like his. How else did I spot him? I recognized the type. None of the others found what they rationalized themselves into thinking they remembered from the time they were Martians. Eventually one of them would stumble onto something. That's coincidence. Not incarnated memory."

She turned her head and blinked at me. I nodded grimly. "I'm an agent," I said. "I go out on the tours for one purpose only—to spot psychos and make sure they don't get out of control. You'd be surprised how many there are. Some of them, like your husband, probably show no sign of instability until they get here. They look around at the evidence of a civilization that existed before *homo sapiens* had evolved on the Earth, and it throws them. If you want to understand more about it read the medical books. They get irrational pre-memories. They look at something and the idea of familiarity associates with the new impression. They look around a corner and see something, and build up the conviction that they had consciously known what was there before they looked around the corner."

I felt that I was making headway with her. I wanted to. I had to.

"You—you say there were others, and they didn't find anything?" she said. She was groping for something logical to grasp. I had to give her that something.

"That's right," I said. "And the law of averages said that someday someone would uncover something that's been missed."

She was nodding slowly now, accepting what I was saying. It was authoritative. She would find confirmation in authoritative books. If she wanted to pursue the subject she would find plenty of evidence, real evidence, to support it. It is a common form of insanity. It was important that she believe that.

We reached the road. C.I. had been prepared. There was a car to take her back to the hotel, a station wagon for Herb who was now very submissive and somewhat dazed, and a third car for me and my precious cargo.

Ten minutes later I was in the Science Building basement, laying the thing on a wooden table, very gently. It seemed solid, each integral part of its form being of a different metal.

None of the men watching me lay it down discounted the danger it contained. They knew too much about how shape and dimension can affect the electronic properties of metal. They knew the thing probably didn't contain an erg of power of its own, but probably triggered and directed the release of cosmic energies as yet unknown to them.

They stared at it. One of them reached out to touch it, then slowly drew his finger back.

I could see the decision crystallizing in their minds behind their serious eyes. This thing would go with the other strange and incomprehensible machines locked in vaults in a concrete building far out on the Martian desert away from the tourist trails of this dead planet. It would remain there until the day when human science advanced far enough to understand it.

"What about the wall in the dome?" I asked.

"They roped it off. They're afraid of it."

"Did you convince his wife he's insane?" one of the science staff asked.

I nodded. "I used the same old line. Told her there were dozens like him, and the law of averages made it certain at least one of them would find something."

He nodded, grinned without humor. "How we love to lie."

I turned away. There was a bitter taste in my mouth from all the lies I'd told—all the bilge.

But I knew the truth, too. I was as sure of that as I was of anything. It wasn't insanity, of course. And it wasn't reincarnation. It seemed to be, because the mind has a habit of *possessing* for its very own anything that enters it.

The truth of the matter was that somehow, in some incomprehensible way, the Martians were still with us. They hated us and they knew how to use our weak ones.

The old Martians—and their science.

I took a last look at the weapon lying on the table, then left the room and climbed the stairs to the first floor. I walked down the silent, empty hall to the exit and out into the night.

I let my eyes roam the blackness of the lifeless Martian desert. With an effort I pulled them away and fixed them on the warmth, the human warmth, beckoning from the hotel.

I started walking toward that bit of comfort, and as I walked the eternal question that haunted all of us in C.I. hovered in the background of my thoughts.

Would we be able to *contain* the Martians until we understood the terrible machines they had left as a deadly heritage?

Tonight we almost hadn't....

I thought of Steve.

FINAL CONTACT

The Hermit of Mars

by Stephen Bartholomew

When Martin Devere was 23 and still working on his Master's, he was hurt by a woman. It was then that he decided that the only things in life worthwhile were pure art and pure science. That, of course, is another story, but it may explain why he chose to become an archeologist in the first place.

Now he was the oldest human being on Mars. He was 91. For many years, in fact, he had been the *only* human being on Mars. Up until today.

He looked through the transparent wall of his pressurized igloo at the puff of dust in the desert where the second rocket had come down. Earth and Mars were just past conjunction, and the regular automatic supply rocket had landed two days ago. As usual, Martin Devere, taking his own good time about it, had unloaded the supplies, keeping the things he really needed and throwing away the useless stuff like the latest microfilmed newspapers and magazines, the taped TV shows and concerts. As payment for his groceries he had then reloaded the rocket with the written reports he had accumulated since the last conjunction, plus a few artifacts.

Then he had pushed a button and sent the rocket on its way again, back to Earth. He didn't mind writing the reports. Most of them were rubbish anyway, but they seemed to keep the people back at the Institute happy. He did mind the artifacts. It seemed wrong to remove them, though he sent only the less valuable ones back. But perhaps it couldn't be helped. One time, the supply rocket had failed to return when he pushed its red button—the thing was still sitting out there in the desert, slowly rusting. Martin Devere had happily unloaded the artifacts and put them back where they belonged. It wasn't his fault.

The puff of dust on the horizon was beginning to settle. This second rocket had descended with a shrill scream through the thin air, its voice more highly pitched than it would have been in denser atmosphere. Martin Devere had looked up from his work in time to see its braking jets vanish behind the low Martian hills a few kilometers distant.

It was much too large to be an automatic supply rocket, even if there had been reason to expect another one. Martin Devere knew it could mean only one thing. Someone was paying him an unannounced visit.

He waited, watching through the igloo wall to see who had come to poke around and bother him after all these years.

At first he was annoyed that the people at the Institute hadn't let him know visitors were coming. Then he reminded himself that it had been years since he'd taken the trouble to listen to his radio receiver, or to read the messages they sent him along with supplies.

After a long time, he made out a smaller dust-puff, and then a little sandcat advancing slowly across the desert. Riding on top of it were two men in space suits.

Everyone on Earth who reads popular magazines or watches TV knows the story of Martin Devere, "The Hermit of Mars." Over the years, now that he is dead, he has become a sort of culture hero, as Dr. Livingston or Albert Schweitzer once were. Though Martin Devere could not be called a humanitarian in any sense of the word. After his divorce from his first and only wife, at the age of 45, he never gave much thought again either to women or any other kind of people—except for his long-dead Martians.

But everyone should know by now how Martin Devere first came to Mars at the age of 50. Even then he was the oldest man on the planet, and Mars sustained quite a large research colony at the time. Only Martin Devere's unchallenged scientific reputation, together with his apparent good health, enabled him to leave Earth as head of a five-man archeological team. This turned up the first fossil ruins far beneath the desert sand.

Then there came a day when the Space Institute of the United Governments decided to abandon Project Mars. It was getting too expensive to maintain. Everything of value to space research had already been learned about the planet, and the archeological site, though yet barely scratched, did not properly come under space research. Closing Project Mars would mean more funds for solar research on Mercury, for the Lunar colony, and for work on the interstellar drive.

So the hundred-odd inhabitants of the Project received orders to leave the igloos and other equipment behind and come back to Earth.

Martin Devere, however, had been on Mars for three years now. When the Project physician gave him his routine exam, it was discovered that a valve in Martin Devere's aorta had developed a faint flutter. Nothing too serious, really. But enough to greatly reduce his chances of surviving another rocket lift-off.

Martin Devere smiled at the news and volunteered to remain behind, alone on Mars. Under the circumstances, the Institute was forced to agree.

On the day that the strange rocket came down behind the desert hills, Martin Devere had been on Mars for a total of 38 years. For the past 35 of them he had been The Hermit, and quite happy about it.

The little sandcat was getting closer. Martin Devere smiled to himself, watching the two men in their clumsy space gear. It was high noon, and a nice comfortable ten degrees centigrade outside. If the two newcomers thought they needed full spacesuits to get around out there, Martin Devere wasn't going to tell them any different. Actually, though the atmospheric pressure was about the same as at the top of Mount Everest, on a beautiful day like this a man could get along easily outdoors with nothing more than an oxygen mask. But let them clomp around in their rubberized long-johns if they wanted to.

In a few minutes they would be coming in through the igloo's airlock. Martin Devere turned away, scowling now. He hoped the Institute hadn't decided to reopen Mars Project. There was plenty of room in all these igloos and connecting tunnels that had been left behind, but with a new expedition here it might get pretty crowded. Mainly, Devere didn't want a bunch of amateurs poking around his diggings, breaking things.

His thumb rubbed slowly across the long stubble on his chin. He wondered if he had made some slip in that last report, or in some of the pictures of the ruins he'd sent back. He'd rather the Institute didn't find out about those fossilized machines he'd dug up. He didn't understand the gadgets himself, but some of the people at the Institute just might decide they were interesting enough to be worth sending up an expert.

The Institute, Devere knew, was interested in machinery, not art objects.

★ ★ ★

One of the men held an automatic pistol pointed at Martin Devere while the other was stripping off his space gear. Then the pistol changed hands while the first man removed his own suit. Martin Devere could have told them that he wasn't afraid of the gun. He didn't actually care much, one way or the other. Martin Devere figured that he had already lived a lot longer, here in this feeble gravity and germ-free, oxygen-rich air, than his tricky heart would have allowed him on Earth. Let them point the gun if they wanted to.

"If you make one move toward the radio transmitter I'll blow your head off," the taller man said. He had black wavy hair that hung over his brow. The other man was completely bald.

"I don't even know if the radio works," Martin Devere answered. "I haven't turned it on in years. I should warn you, though, that if you shoot that thing inside the igloo here, it will puncture the plastic wall and let all the air out. I always keep the pressure up high indoors so I can boil water for coffee."

The tall man frowned in confusion and blinked at the weapon in his hand. Then he stared at the transparent dome above him, as if realizing for the first time that only a thin bubble of plastic separated him from near-vacuum, now that he had removed his suit.

"I was just making some coffee when you showed up," Martin Devere said, turning away. "Have some? I'm afraid it's instant. I've given up trying to get the Institute to send me a can of real coffee in the rocket. They think I need canned TV shows more."

"He's harmless," the bald man said. "You can see he's just an old senile nut. Leave him be, we've work to do."

The tall man lowered his weapon, then let it fall into the holster at his hip.

"No big hurry. I think I'd like some of that coffee first. Say, Pop, how about cooking us a meal in a couple of hours?"

Martin Devere was spooning brown powder into three cups.

"Sure thing. What would you like—beans and franks, or franks and beans?"

★ ★ ★

"I suppose you wonder what we're doing, Pop?" The tall man held the disassembled pieces of his gun in his lap. He was carefully polishing each part with a chemically treated cloth.

It was three days since they had landed, and the tall metal skeleton was beginning to take shape out in the desert. At the moment, the bald man was out alone, testing circuits. Usually the two went out together—they had apparently decided it was safe to leave Martin Devere unguarded, though they had smashed his radio transmitter just in case.

The two men worked steadily during the daylight hours, came back at sunset to eat and sleep, then went out again at dawn. The towering lacework of steel was growing like an ugly flower.

The tall man held the trigger assembly of his gun up to the light. He turned it slowly between his thumb and forefinger. It cast an odd crescent-shaped shadow over the muscles of his jaw.

"No, I don't wonder what you're doing," Martin Devere answered. He was sitting at his workbench, crouched over an ancient metal plate as thin as paper.

The tall man began to put his weapon back together again. He snapped the trigger assembly into the receiver. He pulled the hammer back and then released it; it made a sharp, hard click.

"Not even curious, Pop? Okay, then tell me what *you're* doing. What's that piece of tinfoil you've been staring at the past two hours?"

Martin Devere straightened and turned to look at the other.

"It's an ancient Martian scroll. It's nearly a million years old. I found it in a new pit I've been digging, five hundred meters down. It's the longest and perhaps most important bit of Martian writing I've found so far."

"Yeah? What's it have to say?"

Martin Devere shook his head. "Their language, their whole frame of reference, was fundamentally different from ours. It's something like higher mathematics, you'd have to learn the language to understand it. But I suppose you might say that this is a poem… Yes, an epic poem."

The tall man laughed. He shoved an ammunition magazine into his weapon, pumped a round into the chamber, slipped the gun back into its holster. He got up and began pacing the floor of the igloo. The floor was cluttered with dozens of artifacts.

He stopped and nudged one specimen with his toe.

"What's this thing, Pop? An ancient Martian meatgrinder?"

"I hardly think so. They were vegetarians." He squinted at the object. "I'm afraid I have no idea what it is. It's some sort of machine, but I'm no engineer, I can't imagine what its function was. They—don't build many machines, you know."

The man with the gun turned to stare at Martin Devere.

"You mean *didn't* build, don't you?"

"Yes, of course. Past tense." And Devere turned again to peer at the million-year-old poem before him.

★ ★ ★

"Damn it to hell. This might hold us up a week." The bald man flung the shatterproof helmet of his suit against the igloo wall. His tone of voice was matter-of-fact emotionless. Even the way he threw the helmet betrayed no real emotion. Still wearing the rest of his suit he sat down at Martin Devere's work bench and clenched his fists. His face was smooth, blank.

"What's the matter?" His partner put down some drawings and came over.

"The modulator circuit doesn't check out. I'll have to take the whole works apart and start over again." The bald man spoke—when he did speak—with a faint accent that Martin Devere could not identify.

"It doesn't matter." The other rubbed at his chin. "We're still ahead of our schedule."

"Hey. Old man." The bald man pointed at Devere. "You have anything to drink in this cave of yours?"

Martin Devere frowned, thinking. He remembered a bottle he'd been saving for some special occasion—he couldn't recall what, just now.

"I think I have some bourbon," he said at last. "If I can find it."

"Find it. Mine straight, on the rocks."

When Martin Devere returned awhile later, the bald man was still wearing his helmetless space suit. He and his friend were studying a complex wiring diagram spread out on the work bench.

Martin Devere put two plastic cups down on the bench and poured them full. Neither of the men looked up from their diagram until he had set the bottle down.

"Pour one for yourself, Pop," the tall man said.

"Thanks. Don't mind if I do." Devere went to get another cup. Over his shoulder he said, "Hope you boys don't mind crushed ice instead of cubes. I just set a bucket of water in one of the unheated tunnels for a couple minutes. Then I hit it with a hammer."

It was four hours past sunset, the temperature outside was far below freezing.

"One thing you don't need on Mars is a refrigerator." Pouring himself a drink, the old man suddenly laughed. It was a brief, senile giggle, that made the tall man turn to stare at him.

"Could be uncomfortable, though, if you were ever stuck out there at night." Martin Devere's face was sober once more as he lifted his cup and looked deeply into it. All trace of senility had vanished as suddenly as it had appeared. "Like, say, if you were out there long enough for your suit power to go dead. You'd freeze to a hunk of ice in a few minutes. Me, I never go outside at night."

"Shut up," the bald man said.

★ ★ ★

All day the bald man had been out alone, working on his electronic circuits. Evidently this left his partner nothing to do except study schematics.

Now Martin Devere was aware that his guest had been staring at him for several minutes without speaking. Martin Devere went on polishing the green crystal vase he held in his hand. The vase looked ordinary at first glance, until you noticed that it wasn't quite symmetrical. There was a studied and careful asymmetry about its form, barely discernible, that would disturb you the more you looked at it, until you knew, suddenly, that no human brain could have created that shape.

The polishing cloth moved rhythmically across the vase's curving surfaces. The green crystal reflected light in a way that made you begin to think about boundless seas of water.

"I'll be glad when this job is over with," the tall man said, half aloud.

"When it is, will you go away?" Martin Devere turned the vase slowly in his hands.

"Not for a while yet, Pop." The man with the gun on his hip got to his feet and stretched.

"I don't mind telling you what it's all about, Pop. You're all right. It's simple. My partner and I were sent here by a certain national power that doesn't like being told how to run its own affairs by the United Governments. We're striking the first blow for Freedom. That thing we're putting together out there is a bomb. It could disable most of Earth. It has a new kind of nuclear rocket engine behind it that could carry it across 200 million miles in a few hours.

"You get the idea, Pop? Here on Mars, they won't even find it. And if they did, we could deliver the bomb before they got a missile halfway across. So I hope you won't mind if my partner and I stay a while, Pop."

It was several seconds before Martin Devere answered. He set the crystal vase carefully inside a case and regarded it a moment.

"As long as you don't go messing up my diggings or break any of the artifacts, it's no business of mine."

"And what if I did, Pop?" The tall man walked closer to Martin Devere. He stood over the old man, his shadow on him. His hand rested lightly on the butt of his gun. "What if I were to take all your vases and statues and pots and tablets and smash them to bits, one by one? What would you do then?"

Martin Devere's eyes slowly closed and opened, he made no other move for a minute. Then he got to his feet without looking at the other man. He turned and began to move away, toward a tunnel door that led to the diggings.

Probably the tall man thought that he had finally put the fear of God into Martin Devere. But as he turned back to his pile of schematics he heard the old man's whisper:

"You might regret it."

The man with the gun did not answer.

★ ★ ★

"Tell us about it, Pop."

"Yes, why don't you tell us about it."

They meant Martin Devere's work. The two men had finished their own job. The assembled bomb rested in the desert, silent but alive, like some abnormal growth.

Because of sunspot activity they hadn't yet been able to radio their employers on Earth. The bald man expected conditions to clear in two or three days. When they did clear, he would signal, "The bird is nesting." Then the nation he had mentioned would be ready to deliver its ultimatum to the United Governments.

For the first time since landing on Mars, the two men were idle. They were waiting. They looked as if they were willing to wait a long time if necessary.

Meanwhile, Martin Devere's artifacts were the only amusements available.

Perhaps the old man knew they were making fun of him. But he seemed to take their question seriously. When he began to speak, they found themselves listening.

"We don't know exactly what happened." Martin Devere faced the two men across the cluttered workbench like a lecturer addressing his students. He held in his hand a small bronze statue that might have been a portrayal of one of the old Martian people or, just as likely, some long-extinct animal. In the diffuse sunlight that came through the igloo wall, it cast a shadow on the work bench that was even more disturbingly alien in shape.

"No, we don't know what happened to them," the old man said. "The last of them died nearly a million years ago, before the first Homo Sapiens walked the Earth. From what we—I—have found we know a little about what they were like. But we don't know why they died.

"We do know, for instance, that they never had much interest in technology. Not that they lacked intelligence. They could build a machine when it suited their purposes, whatever those may have been. And I don't say they weren't interested in science. They had a highly developed theoretical science, as sophisticated as their art. You might say they were theoreticians. They were concerned with pure art and pure science—but not with applied technology, or commercialized art.

"My own theory is that they had no need for technology. In the first place, they were vegetarians, not carnivorous. So that their earliest men had no need for hunting weapons or other gadgets. Probably they never developed the aggressive instincts which in humanity led to warfare with its subsequent impetus to applied technology. The Martians never got around to making cars or airplanes or bombs. They dedicated themselves, gentlemen, to the contemplation of beauty.

"Then, nearly a million years ago, something happened to them. Perhaps Mars began to lose her atmosphere then. Her oceans evaporated, the air could no longer retain her heat at night, the farmlands parched and froze. A few of the plant types were able to adapt and survive. But within a few years, all animal life died out. One day, there were suddenly no more Martians left."

Martin Devere's dry, withered hand caressed the small statue he held.

"Who knows? If they'd had time to develop space travel they might have saved themselves. Then again, with a technology like yours, they might have blown themselves up long before the natural catastrophe"

"What do you mean like *yours*?" the tall man said. "You mean like *ours*, don't you?"

But Martin Devere turned away without answering.

★ ★ ★

"Do you have another bottle of bourbon, old man?"

"No, I'm afraid not," Devere said. "There was only that one bottle."

"Too bad. We should have a little celebration." The bald man began sealing himself into his spacesuit.

"I'll wait for you here," his partner said. "I'd better start burning those plans."

Martin Devere looked up from the fragment of ceramic he was cleaning.

"You're going to send the message now?"

Neither of the men bothered to reply, since the answer was self-evident. The bald man tested the air and power equipment of his suit, then turned to his partner a moment before sealing his helmet.

"You checked the sandcat's power supply?"

"Yes, but you'd better take another look at it. I think the battery's leaking."

The bald man nodded and went out the airlock. Martin Devere watched in silence as the other man began to gather up his diagrams and plans and tie them into a neat bundle.

"I guess we can take it easy now, Pop. As soon as that telegram's sent and I get this stuff burned, my partner and I are unemployed. Of course we'll have to hang around a while longer in case they want us to shoot off Baby out there, but there's nothing to that. In the meantime maybe I can help you dig up some more of those old pots and statues."

Martin Devere seemed to be thinking. He watched as the tall man checked to make sure he hadn't forgotten anything, then carried the bundle of plans over to the electronic oven.

"*Baby*. You mean your bomb, out there. You think you might actually shoot it off then."

"Oh, maybe, maybe not."

"Couldn't they fire it from Earth by radio?" Devere asked.

"Nope. Somebody might try jamming."

"Oh, I see...."

Martin Devere was silent again until the tall man opened the oven and removed a bundle of gray ash. He dumped the ashes into a bucket and began stirring them with his hand.

"Something else I was wondering about," Devere said. He began cleaning the fragment of ceramic again, his hands working in a slow circular motion.

"Supposing the United Governments find out where the bomb is. They might send a missile to blow it up."

"Told you, Pop. Baby can out-run anything else that flies. Wouldn't do them any good."

"Yes, yes. Still, the missile would hit Mars, wouldn't it? I mean, it would destroy all this—the igloos, my diggings…"

The tall man gave a laugh.

"Don't worry so much, Pop. We'd have plenty of time to get in the ship and clear out. We might even take you with us."

"Still…" But the old man lapsed again into thought.

★ ★ ★

An hour later, the short-range radio gave a shrill beep. The tall man went over and flipped the *talk* switch.

"Yeah?"

"Hello. Listen, I did something stupid."

Martin Devere looked up at the sound of the bald man's voice. Devere's hands still held the piece of ceramic. He had polished it until a complex geometric design was visible, etched in reds and blues. It might have been equally a decoration or some mechanical diagram.

"Did you get the message sent?" the tall man asked.

"Yes, that part's all right. I got to the ship and contacted headquarters. I think they're going to deliver the ultimatum right away. Now we just wait for orders. The only thing is, the sandcat's power went dead on me while I was halfway down a hill. It started to roll. I jumped out. This low gravity fooled me and I think I've broken my ankle, it hurts like hell."

The tall man cursed in a low voice.

"All right, all right," he said after a moment. "Just take it easy. I'll have to come out and get you."

"I think the sandcat is all right. Stupid of me to jump like that, wasn't thinking. Better bring a spare battery with you. Oh, and you'd better bring a light too. It will be getting dark in another half hour."

"Okay, just wait for me. I'll home in on your suit radio."

The tall man switched off the receiver and went to his own suit locker. Martin Devere watched as he removed the holster and weapon from his hip. He pulled the heavy plastic trousers over his denim jumper and then buckled the gun back again before starting on the rest of the spacesuit.

"Nothing serious, I hope?" Martin Devere put the ceramic down carefully and picked up another object from a stack of artifacts.

"You heard, didn't you? You any good at setting a broken ankle, Pop?"

"Oh, I could manage, I guess. Broke my arm down in the diggings once. Had to set it myself. Twenty years ago, I think it was. I've been more careful since then."

He gave a laugh. It started as a normal laugh, then broke to a senile giggle. Then his face was serious again. He carried the new artifact closer to the man with the gun.

"You remember, I was telling you, the Martians were vegetarians. They never made any weapons for hunting. They did know about explosives, though."

"What's that thing?" The tall man, struggling with the buckles of his breathing equipment, glanced at the object in Devere's hands. It looked like badly corroded bronze, and consisted of a long tube with a large bulb at one end.

"This? Oh, this is some kind of a tool I found. I think it was a digging tool, used for breaking up rocks. They *did* build canals, you know. As I was saying, they knew about explosives. This tool, for instance. It worked by means of a small, shaped charge inside this bulb here. The explosion was so well-focused that there was almost no recoil. A high-energy shock wave was emitted from the barrel. Very effective at short range. But the most amazing thing about this tool is that the chemical explosive is still potent after lying underground for nearly a million years.

"Oh, by the way. There's nothing wrong with your sandcat's battery. It was the motor I sabotaged."

Then Martin Devere pointed the ancient digging tool at the tall man and blew him into two neat pieces.

★ ★ ★

The Hermit of Mars never did get around to walking out to the space ship and using his visitor's radio to tell Earth what had happened. He really intended to, but he forgot. The ultimatum that was delivered to the United Governments failed, of course, but no one knew exactly why until the next Earth-Mars conjunction.

The United Governments was prevailed on by the World Television Service to send out someone to interview the Hermit, if he were still alive.

That interview was unfortunate. It might have established Martin Devere as the world hero that he was, and he might have been awarded some kind of medal. As it went, his rude and insulting answers to the young man's questions made him unpopular for years.

His last answer in the interview was the worst. The young man, already sweating, looked in desperation at the green crystal vase that Martin Devere insisted on holding in front of the television lens. Back at the Institute, a dozen faces were flushing red with indignation as their owners realized what the old man had been holding back.

"Tell me, Dr. Devere," the young man asked. "You seem a very modest man. Doesn't it make you the least bit proud to know that you've saved the world?"

Martin Devere lowered his vase and gave the young man a puzzled look.

"You mean Earth? Tell me, why should I want to save *that* world?"

The Man Who Hated Mars

by Randall Garrett

"I want you to put me in prison!" the big, hairy man said in a trembling voice.

He was addressing his request to a thin woman sitting behind a desk that seemed much too big for her. The plaque on the desk said:

LT. PHOEBE HARRIS
TERRAN REHABILITATION SERVICE

Lieutenant Harris glanced at the man before her for only a moment before she returned her eyes to the dossier on the desk; but long enough to verify the impression his voice had given. Ron Clayton was a big, ugly, cowardly, dangerous man.

He said: "Well? Dammit, say something!"

The lieutenant raised her eyes again. "Just be patient until I've read this." Her voice and eyes were expressionless, but her hand moved beneath the desk.

Clayton froze. *She's yellow!* he thought. She's turned on the trackers! He could see the pale greenish glow of their little eyes watching him all around the room. If he made any fast move, they would cut him down with a stun beam before he could get two feet.

She had thought he was going to jump her. *Little rat!* he thought, *somebody ought to slap her down!*

He watched her check through the heavy dossier in front of her. Finally, she looked up at him again.

"Clayton, your last conviction was for strong-arm robbery. You were given a choice between prison on Earth and freedom here on Mars. You picked Mars."

He nodded slowly. He'd been broke and hungry at the time. A sneaky little rat named Johnson had bilked Clayton out of his fair share of the Corey payroll job, and Clayton had been forced to get the money somehow. He hadn't mussed the guy up much; besides, it was the sucker's own fault. If he hadn't tried to yell—

Lieutenant Harris went on: "I'm afraid you can't back down now."

"But it isn't fair! The most I'd have got on that frame-up would've been ten years. I've been here fifteen already!"

"I'm sorry, Clayton. It can't be done. You're here. Period. Forget about trying to get back. Earth doesn't want you." Her voice sounded choppy, as though she were trying to keep it calm.

Clayton broke into a whining rage. "You can't do that! It isn't fair! I never did anything to you! I'll go talk to the Governor! He'll listen to reason! You'll see! I'll—"

"*Shut up!*" the woman snapped harshly. "I'm getting sick of it! I personally think you should have been locked up—permanently. I think this idea of forced colonization is going to breed trouble for Earth someday, but it is about the only way you can get anybody to colonize this frozen hunk of mud.

"Just keep it in mind that I don't like it any better than you do—*and I didn't strong-arm anybody to deserve the assignment!* Now get out of here!"

She moved a hand threateningly toward the manual controls of the stun beam.

Clayton retreated fast. The trackers ignored anyone walking away from the desk; they were set only to spot threatening movements toward it.

Outside the Rehabilitation Service Building, Clayton could feel the tears running down the inside of his face mask. He'd asked again and again—God only knew how many times—in the past fifteen years. Always the same answer. No.

When he'd heard that this new administrator was a woman, he'd hoped she might be easier to convince. She wasn't. If anything, she was harder than the others.

The heat-sucking frigidity of the thin Martian air whispered around him in a feeble breeze. He shivered a little and began walking toward the recreation center.

There was a high, thin piping in the sky above him which quickly became a scream in the thin air.

He turned for a moment to watch the ship land, squinting his eyes to see the number on the hull.

Fifty-two. Space Transport Ship Fifty-two.

Probably bringing another load of poor suckers to freeze to death on Mars.

That was the thing he hated about Mars—the cold. The everlasting damned cold! And the oxidation pills; take one every three hours or smother in the poor, thin air.

The government could have put up domes; it could have put in building-to-building tunnels, at least. It could have done a hell of a lot of things to make Mars a decent place for human beings.

But no—the government had other ideas. A bunch of bigshot scientific characters had come up with the idea nearly twenty-three years before. Clayton could remember the words on the sheet he had been given when he was sentenced.

"Mankind is inherently an adaptable animal. If we are to colonize the planets of the Solar System, we must meet the conditions on those planets as best we can.

"Financially, it is impracticable to change an entire planet from its original condition to one which will support human life as it exists on Terra.

"But man, since he is adaptable, can change himself—modify his structure slightly—so that he can live on these planets with only a minimum of change in the environment."

So they made you live outside and like it. So you froze and you choked and you suffered.

Clayton hated Mars. He hated the thin air and the cold. More than anything, he hated the cold.

Ron Clayton wanted to go home.

The Recreation Building was just ahead; at least it would be warm inside. He pushed in through the outer and inner doors, and he heard the burst of music from the jukebox. His stomach tightened up into a hard cramp.

They were playing Heinlein's *Green Hills of Earth*.

There was almost no other sound in the room, although it was full of people. There were plenty of colonists who claimed to like Mars, but even they were silent when that song was played.

Clayton wanted to go over and smash the machine—make it stop reminding him. He clenched his teeth and his fists and his eyes and cursed mentally. *God, how I hate Mars!*

When the hauntingly nostalgic last chorus faded away, he walked over to the machine and fed it full of enough coins to keep it going on something else until he left.

At the bar, he ordered a beer and used it to wash down another oxidation tablet. It wasn't good beer; it didn't even deserve the name. The atmospheric pressure was so low as to boil all the carbon dioxide out of it, so the brewers never put it back in after fermentation.

He was sorry for what he had done—really and truly sorry. If they'd only give him one more chance, he'd make good. Just one more chance. He'd work things out.

He'd promised himself that both times they'd put him up before, but things had been different then. He hadn't really been given another chance, what with parole boards and all.

Clayton closed his eyes and finished the beer. He ordered another.

He'd worked in the mines for fifteen years. It wasn't that he minded work really, but the foreman had it in for him. Always giving him a bad time; always picking out the lousy jobs for him.

Like the time he'd crawled into a side-boring in Tunnel 12 for a nap during lunch and the foreman had caught him. When he promised never to do it again if the foreman wouldn't put it on report, the guy said, "Yeah. Sure. Hate to hurt a guy's record."

Then he'd put Clayton on report anyway. Strictly a rat.

Not that Clayton ran any chance of being fired; they never fired anybody. But they'd fined him a day's pay. A whole day's pay.

He tapped his glass on the bar, and the barman came over with another beer. Clayton looked at it, then up at the barman. "Put a head on it."

The bartender looked at him sourly. "I've got some soapsuds here, Clayton, and one of these days I'm gonna put some in your beer if you keep pulling that gag."

That was the trouble with some guys. No sense of humor.

Somebody came in the door and then somebody else came in behind him, so that both inner and outer doors were open for an instant. A blast of icy breeze struck Clayton's back, and he shivered. He started to say something, then changed his mind; the doors were already closed again, and besides, one of the guys was bigger than he was.

The iciness didn't seem to go away immediately. It was like the mine. Little old Mars was cold clear down to her core—or at least down as far as they'd drilled. The walls were frozen and seemed to radiate a chill that pulled the heat right out of your blood.

Somebody was playing *Green Hills* again, damn them. Evidently all of his own selections had run out earlier than he'd thought they would.

Hell! There was nothing to do here. He might as well go home.

"Gimme another beer, Mac."

He'd go home as soon as he finished this one.

He stood there with his eyes closed, listening to the music and hating Mars.

A voice next to him said: "I'll have a whiskey."

The voice sounded as if the man had a bad cold, and Clayton turned slowly to look at him. After all the sterilization they went through before they left Earth, nobody on Mars ever had a cold, so there was only one thing that would make a man's voice sound like that.

Clayton was right. The fellow had an oxygen tube clamped firmly over his nose. He was wearing the uniform of the Space Transport Service.

"Just get in on the ship?" Clayton asked conversationally.

The man nodded and grinned. "Yeah. Four hours before we take off again." He poured down the whiskey. "Sure cold out."

Clayton agreed. "It's always cold." He watched enviously as the spaceman ordered another whiskey.

Clayton couldn't afford whiskey. He probably could have by this time, if the mines had made him a foreman, like they should have.

Maybe he could talk the spaceman out of a couple of drinks.

"My name's Clayton. Ron Clayton."

The spaceman took the offered hand. "Mine's Parkinson, but everybody calls me Parks."

"Sure, Parks. Uh—can I buy you a beer?"

Parks shook his head. "No, thanks. I started on whiskey. Here, let me buy you one."

"Well—thanks. Don't mind if I do."

They drank them in silence, and Parks ordered two more.

"Been here long?" Parks asked.

"Fifteen years. Fifteen long, long years."

"Did you—uh—I mean—" Parks looked suddenly confused.

Clayton glanced quickly to make sure the bartender was out of earshot. Then he grinned. "You mean am I a convict? Nah. I came here because I wanted to. But—" He lowered his voice. "—we don't talk about it around here. You know." He gestured with one hand—a gesture that took in everyone else in the room.

Parks glanced around quickly, moving only his eyes. "Yeah. I see," he said softly.

"This your first trip?" asked Clayton.

"First one to Mars. Been on the Luna run a long time."

"Low pressure bother you much?"

"Not much. We only keep it at six pounds in the ships. Half helium and half oxygen. Only thing that bothers me is the oxy here. Or rather, the oxy that *isn't* here." He took a deep breath through his nose tube to emphasize his point.

Clayton clamped his teeth together, making the muscles at the side of his jaw stand out.

Parks didn't notice. "You guys have to take those pills, don't you?"

"Yeah."

"I had to take them once. Got stranded on Luna. The cat I was in broke down eighty some miles from Aristarchus Base and I had to walk back—with my oxy low. Well, I figured—"

Clayton listened to Parks' story with a great show of attention, but he had heard it before. This "lost on the moon" stuff and its variations had been going the rounds for forty years. Every once in a while, it actually did happen to someone; just often enough to keep the story going.

This guy did have a couple of new twists, but not enough to make the story worthwhile.

"Boy," Clayton said when Parks had finished, "you were lucky to come out of that alive!"

Parks nodded, well pleased with himself, and bought another round of drinks.

"Something like that happened to me a couple of years ago," Clayton began. "I'm supervisor on the third shift in the mines at Xanthe, but at the time, I was only a foreman. One day, a couple of guys went to a branch tunnel to—"

It was a very good story. Clayton had made it up himself, so he knew that Parks had never heard it before. It was gory in just the right places, with a nice effect at the end.

"—so I had to hold up the rocks with my back while the rescue crew pulled the others out of the tunnel by crawling between my legs. Finally, they got some steel beams down there to take the load off, and I could let go. I was in the hospital for a week," he finished.

Parks was nodding vaguely. Clayton looked up at the clock above the bar and realized that they had been talking for better than an hour. Parks was buying another round.

Parks was a hell of a nice fellow.

There was, Clayton found, only one trouble with Parks. He got to talking so loud that the bartender refused to serve either one of them any more drinks.

The bartender said Clayton was getting loud, too, but it was just because he had to talk loud to make Parks hear him.

Clayton helped Parks put his mask and parka on and they walked out into the cold night.

Parks began to sing *Green Hills*. About halfway through, he stopped and turned to Clayton.

"I'm from Indiana."

Clayton had already spotted him as an American by his accent.

"Indiana? That's nice. Real nice."

"Yeah. You talk about green hills, we got green hills in Indiana. What time is it?"

Clayton told him.

"Jeez-krise! Ol' spaship takes off in an hour. Ought to have one more drink first."

Clayton realized he didn't like Parks. But maybe he'd buy a bottle.

Sharkie Johnson worked in Fuels Section, and he made a nice little sideline of stealing alcohol, cutting it, and selling it. He thought it was real funny to call it Martian Gin.

Clayton said: "Let's go over to Sharkie's. Sharkie will sell us a bottle."

"Okay," said Parks. "We'll get a bottle. That's what we need: a bottle."

It was quite a walk to the Shark's place. It was so cold that even Parks was beginning to sober up a little. He was laughing like hell when Clayton started to sing.

"We're going over to the Shark's to buy a jug of gin for Parks! Hi ho, hi ho, hi ho!"

One thing about a few drinks; you didn't get so cold. You didn't feel it too much, anyway.

★ ★ ★

The Shark still had his light on when they arrived. Clayton whispered to Parks: "I'll go in. He knows me. He wouldn't sell it if you were around. You got eight credits?"

"Sure I got eight credits. Just a minute, and I'll give you eight credits." He fished around for a minute inside his parka, and pulled out his notecase. His gloved fingers were a little clumsy, but he managed to get out a five and three ones and hand them to Clayton.

"You wait out here," Clayton said.

He went in through the outer door and knocked on the inner one. He should have asked for ten credits. Sharkie only charged five, and that would leave him three for himself. But he could have got ten—maybe more.

When he came out with the bottle, Parks was sitting on a rock, shivering.

"Jeez-krise!" he said. "It's cold out here. Let's get to someplace where it's warm."

"Sure. I got the bottle. Want a drink?"

Parks took the bottle, opened it, and took a good belt out of it.

"Hooh!" he breathed. "Pretty smooth."

As Clayton drank, Parks said: "Hey! I better get back to the field! I know! We can go to the men's room and finish the bottle before the ship takes off! Isn't that a good idea? It's warm there."

They started back down the street toward the spacefield.

"Yep, I'm from Indiana. Southern part, down around Bloomington," Parks said. "Gimme the jug. Not Bloomington, Illinois—Bloomington, Indiana. We really got green hills down there." He drank, and handed the bottle back to Clayton. "Pers-nally, I don't see why anybody'd stay on Mars. Here y'are, practic'ly on the equator in the middle of the summer, and it's colder than hell. Brrr!

"Now if you was smart, you'd go home, where it's warm. Mars wasn't built for people to live on, anyhow. I don't see how you stand it."

That was when Clayton decided he really hated Parks.

And when Parks said: "Why be dumb, friend? Whyn't you go home?" Clayton kicked him in the stomach, hard.

"And that's, that—" Clayton said as Parks doubled over.

He said it again as he kicked him in the head. And in the ribs. Parks was gasping as he writhed on the ground, but he soon lay still.

Then Clayton saw why. Parks' nose tube had come off when Clayton's foot struck his head.

Parks was breathing heavily, but he wasn't getting any oxygen.

That was when the Big Idea hit Ron Clayton. With a nosepiece on like that, you couldn't tell who a man was. He took another drink from the jug and then began to take Parks' clothes off.

The uniform fit Clayton fine, and so did the nose mask. He dumped his own clothing on top of Parks' nearly nude body, adjusted the little oxygen tank so that the gas would flow properly through the mask, took the first deep breath of good air he'd had in fifteen years, and walked toward the spacefield.

He went into the men's room at the Port Building, took a drink, and felt in the pockets of the uniform for Parks' identification. He found it and opened the booklet. It read:

PARKINSON, HERBERT J.
Steward 2nd Class, STS

Above it was a photo, and a set of fingerprints.

Clayton grinned. They'd never know it wasn't Parks getting on the ship.

Parks was a steward, too. A cook's helper. That was good. If he'd been a jetman or something like that, the crew might wonder why he wasn't on duty at takeoff. But a steward was different.

Clayton sat for several minutes, looking through the booklet and drinking from the bottle. He emptied it just before the warning sirens keened through the thin air.

Clayton got up and went outside toward the ship.

★ ★ ★

"Wake up! Hey, you! Wake up!"

Somebody was slapping his cheeks. Clayton opened his eyes and looked at the blurred face over his own.

From a distance, another voice said: "Who is it?"

The blurred face said: "I don't know. He was asleep behind these cases. I think he's drunk."

Clayton wasn't drunk—he was sick. His head felt like hell. Where the devil was he?

"Get up, bud. Come on, get up!"

Clayton pulled himself up by holding to the man's arm. The effort made him dizzy and nauseated.

The other man said: "Take him down to sick bay, Casey. Get some thiamin into him."

Clayton didn't struggle as they led him down to the sick bay. He was trying to clear his head. Where was he? He must have been pretty drunk last night.

He remembered meeting Parks. And getting thrown out by the bartender. Then what?

Oh, yeah. He'd gone to the Shark's for a bottle. From there on, it was mostly gone. He remembered a fight or something, but that was all that registered.

The medic in the sick bay fired two shots from a hypo-gun into both arms, but Clayton ignored the slight sting.

"Where am I?"

"Real original. Here, take these." He handed Clayton a couple of capsules, and gave him a glass of water to wash them down with.

When the water hit his stomach, there was an immediate reaction.

"Oh, Christ!" the medic said. "Get a mop, somebody. Here, bud; heave into this." He put a basin on the table in front of Clayton.

It took them the better part of an hour to get Clayton awake enough to realize what was going on and where he was. Even then, he was plenty groggy.

★ ★ ★

It was the First Officer of the STS-52 who finally got the story straight. As soon as Clayton was in condition, the medic and the quartermaster officer who had found him took him up to the First Officer's compartment.

"I was checking through the stores this morning when I found this man. He was asleep, dead drunk, behind the crates."

"He was drunk, all right," supplied the medic. "I found this in his pocket." He flipped a booklet to the First Officer.

The First was a young man, not older than twenty-eight with tough-looking gray eyes. He looked over the booklet.

"Where did you get Parkinson's ID booklet? And his uniform?"

Clayton looked down at his clothes in wonder. "I don't know."

"You *don't know?* That's a hell of an answer."

"Well, I was drunk," Clayton said defensively. "A man doesn't know what he's doing when he's drunk." He frowned in concentration. He knew he'd have to think up some story.

"I kind of remember we made a bet. I bet him I could get on the ship. Sure—I remember, now. That's what happened; I bet him I could get on the ship and we traded clothes."

"Where is he now?"

"At my place, sleeping it off, I guess."

"Without his oxy-mask?"

"Oh, I gave him my oxidation pills for the mask."

The First shook his head. "That sounds like the kind of trick Parkinson would pull, all right. I'll have to write it up and turn you both in to the authorities when we hit Earth." He eyed Clayton. "What's your name?"

"Cartwright. Sam Cartwright," Clayton said without batting an eye.

"Volunteer or convicted colonist?"

"Volunteer."

The First looked at him for a long moment, disbelief in his eyes.

It didn't matter. Volunteer or convict, there was no place Clayton could go. From the officer's viewpoint, he was as safely imprisoned in the spaceship as he would be on Mars or a prison on Earth.

The First wrote in the log book, and then said: "Well, we're one man short in the kitchen. You wanted to take Parkinson's place; brother, you've got it—without pay." He paused for a moment.

"You know, of course," he said judiciously, "that you'll be shipped back to Mars immediately. And you'll have to work out your passage both ways—it will be deducted from your pay."

Clayton nodded. "I know."

"I don't know what else will happen. If there's a conviction, you may lose your volunteer status on Mars. And there may be fines taken out of your pay, too.

"Well, that's all, Cartwright. You can report to Kissman in the kitchen."

The First pressed a button on his desk and spoke into the intercom. "Who was on duty at the airlock when the crew came aboard last night? Send him up. I want to talk to him."

Then the quartermaster officer led Clayton out the door and took him to the kitchen.

The ship's driver tubes were pushing it along at a steady five hundred centimeters per second squared acceleration, pushing her steadily closer to Earth with a little more than half a gravity of drive.

★ ★ ★

There wasn't much for Clayton to do, really. He helped to select the foods that went into the automatics, and he cleaned them out after each meal was cooked. Once every day, he had to partially dismantle them for a really thorough going-over.

And all the time, he was thinking.

Parkinson must be dead; he knew that. That meant the Chamber. And even if he wasn't, they'd send Clayton back to Mars. Luckily, there was no way for either planet to communicate with the ship; it was hard enough to keep a beam trained on a planet without trying to hit such a comparatively small thing as a ship.

But they would know about it on Earth by now. They would pick him up the instant the ship landed. And the best he could hope for was a return to Mars.

No, by God! He wouldn't go back to that frozen mud-ball! He'd stay on Earth, where it was warm and comfortable and a man could live where he was meant to live. Where there was plenty of air to breathe and plenty of water to drink. Where the beer tasted like beer and not like slop. Earth. Good green hills, the like of which exists nowhere else.

Slowly, over the days, he evolved a plan. He watched and waited and checked each little detail to make sure nothing would go wrong. It *couldn't* go wrong. He didn't want to die, and he didn't want to go back to Mars.

Nobody on the ship liked him; they couldn't appreciate his position. He hadn't done anything to them, but they just didn't like him. He didn't know why; he'd *tried* to get along with them. Well, if they didn't like him, the hell with them.

If things worked out the way he figured, they'd be damned sorry.

He was very clever about the whole plan. When turn-over came, he pretended to get violently space sick. That gave him an opportunity to steal a bottle of chloral hydrate from the medic's locker.

And, while he worked in the kitchen, he spent a great deal of time sharpening a big carving knife.

Once, during his off time, he managed to disable one of the ship's two lifeboats. He was saving the other for himself.

★ ★ ★

The ship was eight hours out from Earth and still decelerating when Clayton pulled his getaway.

It was surprisingly easy. He was supposed to be asleep when he sneaked down to the drive compartment with the knife. He pushed open the door, looked in, and grinned like an ape.

The Engineer and the two jetmen were out cold from the chloral hydrate in the coffee from the kitchen.

Moving rapidly, he went to the spares locker and began methodically to smash every replacement part for the drivers. Then he took three of the signal bombs from the emergency kit, set them for five minutes, and placed them around the driver circuits.

He looked at the three sleeping men. What if they woke up before the bombs went off? He didn't want to kill them though. He wanted them to know what had happened and who had done it.

He grinned. There was a way. He simply had to drag them outside and jam the door lock. He took the key from the Engineer, inserted it, turned it, and snapped off the head, leaving the body of the key still in the lock. Nobody would unjam it in the next four minutes.

Then he began to run up the stairwell toward the good lifeboat.

He was panting and out of breath when he arrived, but no one had stopped him. No one had even seen him.

He clambered into the lifeboat, made everything ready, and waited.

The signal bombs were not heavy charges; their main purposes was to make a flare bright enough to be seen for thousands of miles in space. Fluorine and magnesium made plenty of light—and heat.

Quite suddenly, there was no gravity. He had felt nothing, but he knew that the bombs had exploded. He punched the LAUNCH switch on the control board of the lifeboat, and the little ship leaped out from the side of the greater one.

Then he turned on the drive, set it at half a gee, and watched the STS-52 drop behind him. It was no longer decelerating, so it would miss Earth and drift on into space. On the other hand, the lifeship would come down very neatly within a few hundred miles of the spaceport in Utah, the destination of the STS-52.

Landing the lifeship would be the only difficult part of the maneuver, but they were designed to be handled by beginners. Full instructions were printed on the simplified control board.

Clayton studied them for a while, then set the alarm to waken him in seven hours and dozed off to sleep.

He dreamed of Indiana. It was full of nice, green hills and leafy woods, and Parkinson was inviting him over to his mother's house for chicken and whiskey. And all for free.

Beneath the dream was the calm assurance that they would never catch him and send him back. When the STS-52 failed to show up, they would think he had been lost with it. They would never look for him.

When the alarm rang, Earth was a mottled globe looming hugely beneath the ship. Clayton watched the dials on the board, and began to follow the instructions on the landing sheet.

He wasn't too good at it. The accelerometer climbed higher and higher, and he felt as though he could hardly move his hands to the proper switches.

He was less than fifteen feet off the ground when his hand slipped. The ship, out of control, shifted, spun, and toppled over on its side, smashing a great hole in the cabin.

Clayton shook his head and tried to stand up in the wreckage. He got to his hands and knees, dizzy but unhurt, and took a deep breath of the fresh air that was blowing in through the hole in the cabin.

It felt just like home.

★ ★ ★

Criminal Investigation Bureau
Regional Headquarters
Cheyenne, Wyoming
20 January 2102
To: P. D. Latimer, Space Transport Service
Subject: Lifeship 2, STS-52

Dear Paul,

I have on hand the copies of your reports on the rescue of the men on the disabled STS-52. It is fortunate that the lunar radar stations could compute their orbit.

The detailed official report will follow, but briefly, this is what happened:

The lifeship landed—or, rather, crashed—several miles west of Cheyenne, as you know, but it was impossible to find the man who was piloting it until yesterday because of the weather.

He has been identified as Ronald Watkins Clayton, exiled to Mars fifteen years ago.

Evidently, he didn't realize that fifteen years of Martian gravity had so weakened his muscles that he could hardly walk under the pull of a full Earth gee.

As it was, he could only crawl about a hundred yards from the wrecked lifeship before he collapsed.

Well, I hope this clears up everything. I hope you're not getting the snow storms up there like we've been getting them.

John B. Remley
Captain, CBI

Say "Hello" for Me

by Frank W. Coggins

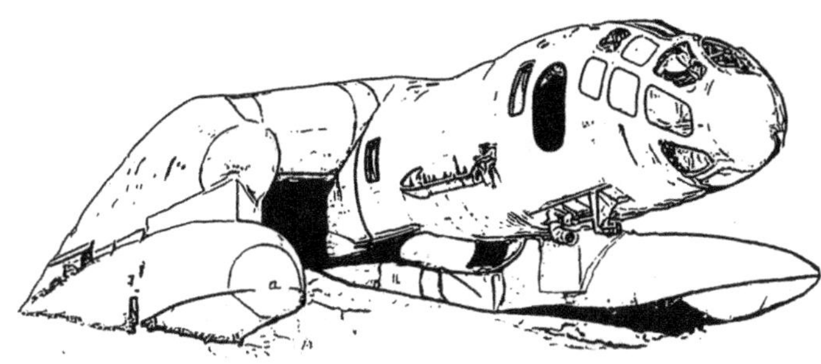

This was to be *the day*, but of course Professor Pettibone had no way of knowing it. He arose, as he had been doing for the previous twenty years, donned the tattered remnants of his space suit, and went out into the open. He stood erect, bronzed, magnificent, faced distant Earth, and recited:

"Good morning, bright sunshine, we're glad you are here. You make the world happy and bring us good cheer."

It was something he had heard as a child and, isolated here on Mars, he had remembered it and used it to keep from losing his power of speech.

The ritual finished, he walked to the edge of the nearest canal, and gathered a bushel or so of dried Martian moss. He returned and began polishing the shiny exterior of the wrecked space ship. It had to really glitter if it was to be an effective beacon in guiding the rescue ship.

Professor Pettibone knew—had known for years—that a ship would come. It was just a matter of time, and as the years slipped by, his faith diminished not a whit.

With his task half completed, he glanced up at the sun and quickened the polishing. It was a long walk to the place the berry bushes grew, and if he arrived too late, the sun would have dried out the night's crop of fragile berries and he would wait until the morrow for nourishment.

But on this day, he was fated to not visit the bush area. An alien sound from above drew the Professor's eyes from his work, and he knew that *the day* had arrived.

The ship was three times as large as any he had ever visualized, and its futuristic design told him, sharply, how far he had fallen behind in his dreaming. He smiled and said, quite calmly, "I daresay I am about to be rescued."

And he experienced a thrill as the great ship set down and two men emerged therefrom. A thrill tinged with a sense of guilt, because emotional experiences were rare in an isolated life and seemed somehow indecent.

The two men held weapons. They advanced upon Professor Pettibone, looked up into his face, and reflected a certain wary hostility. That the hostility was tinged with instinctive respect, even awe, made it no less potent.

One of them asked, "Fella—man came in ship—sky boat—long time ago. Him dead? Where?" Appropriate gestures accompanied the words.

Professor Pettibone smiled down at the little men and bowed. "You are of course referring to me. I came in the ship. I am Professor Pettibone. It was nice of you to hunt me up."

The eyes of the two Terran spacemen met and locked in startled inquiry. One of them voiced the reaction of both when he said, "What the hell—"

"You no doubt are curious as to the fate of the other members of the expedition. They were killed, all save Fletcher, who lasted a week." Professor Pettibone waved a hand. "There, in the graveyard."

But their eyes remained on the only survivor of that ill-fated first expedition. It was hard to accept him as the man they sought, but, faced with undeniable similarity between what they expected and what they had found, the two spacemen had no alternative.

"I hope your food supply is ample and varied," Professor Pettibone said.

This seemed to bring them out of their bemusement. "Of course, Professor. Would you care to come aboard?"

The other made a try at congenial levity. "You must be pretty hungry after twenty years."

"Really? Has it been that long? I tried to keep track at first..."

"We can blast off anytime you say. You're probably pretty anxious to get back."

"Indeed, I am. The changes, in twenty years must be breathtaking. I wonder if they'll remember me."

A short time later, the Professor said, "It's amazing. A ship of this size handled by only two men." Then he sat down to a repast laid out by one of the awed spacemen.

But, after nibbling a bit of this, a forkful of that, he found that satisfaction lay in the anticipation more so than in the eating.

"We'll look around and see what we can find in the way of clothing for you, Professor," one of the spacemen said. Then the man's bemusement returned. His eyes traveled over the magnificent physique before him. The perfect giant of a man;

the great, Apollo-like head with the calm, clear eyes; the expression of complete contentment and serenity.

The space man said, "Professor, to what do you attribute the changes in your body? What is there about this planet?"

"I really don't know." Professor Pettibone looked down his torso with an impersonal eye. "I think the greenish skin pigmentation is a result of mineral-heavy vapors that occur during certain seasons. As to my body's growth, I haven't a clue."

But the two spacemen, though they didn't refer to it, were not concerned with the body so much as the aura of completeness, the radiation of contentment which came from somewhere within.

And it was passing strange that nothing more was said about the Professor returning to Earth. No great revelation, suddenly arrived at, that he would not go. Rather, they discussed various things that three gentlemen, meeting casually, would discuss.

Then Professor Pettibone arose from his chair and said, "It was kind of you to drop off and see me."

And one of the spacemen replied, "A pleasure, sir. A real pleasure indeed."

Then the Professor left the ship and watched it lift up on a tail of red fire and go away. He raised an arm and waved. "Say 'hello' for me," he called. Then he turned away and, from force of habit, he began again to polish the hull, knowing that he would keep it shining, and be proud of it, for many years to come.

★ ★ ★

Almost beyond reach of the planet, one of the spacemen flipped a switch and put certain sensitive communication mechanisms to work. So sensitive, they could pick up etheric vibrations far away and make them audible.

But only faintly, came the pleasant voice of a contented man:

"Good morning, bright sunshine, we're glad you are here. You make the world…"